✱

B... ... ...is Best

Strange and startling stories . . . lightning-quick dialogue . . . a crackling style that keeps the action moving almost faster than the story can be read—these are the trademarks of Alfred Bester, one of the most inventive authors in the field today.

Here, for the first time in book form, is a galaxy of Bester's outstanding stories, including: **Fondly Fahrenheit:** a killer robot and his master flee from the planetary police . . . **Disappearing Act:** a U.S. army hospital is faced with an insolvable problem—patients who disappear and reappear at will . . . **Of Time and Third Avenue:** a 1950 man comes into possession of a 1990 almanac, and finds that in order to keep it he must match wits with a man from the future . . . **Oddy and Id:** a charming but diabolical monster has the power to rule the world . . . **The Roller Coaster:** a girl from the future has an affair with a twentieth-century man . . . **Adam and No Eve:** he was the last man on earth, the sole survivor of a total, chain-reaction holocaust.

Other SIGNET Science Fiction

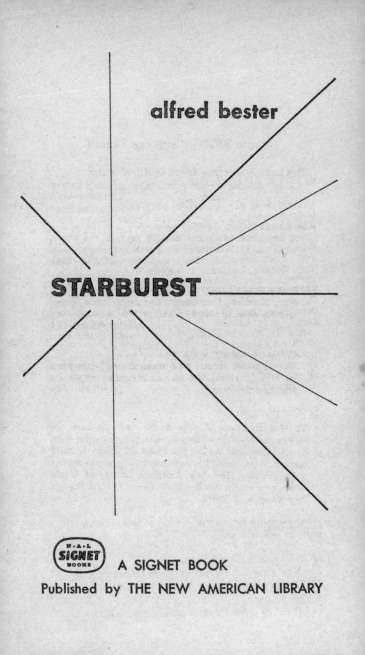

alfred bester

STARBURST

N·A·L
SIGNET
BOOKS
A SIGNET BOOK
Published by THE NEW AMERICAN LIBRARY

SIGNET TRADEMARK REG. U.S. PAT. OFF. AND FOREIGN COUNTRIES
REGISTERED TRADEMARK—MARCA REGISTRADA
HECHO EN CHICAGO, U.S.A.

SIGNET BOOKS are published by
The New American Library of World Literature, Inc.
501 Madison Avenue, New York, New York 10022

PRINTED IN THE UNITED STATES OF AMERICA

Contents

To
ANTHONY BOUCHER
and
J. FRANCIS McCOMAS

Disappearing Act

THIS ONE WASN'T THE LAST WAR OR A WAR TO END war. They called it the War for the American Dream. General Carpenter struck that note and sounded it constantly.

There are fighting generals (vital to an army), political generals (vital to an administration), and public relations generals (vital to a war). General Carpenter was a master of public relations. Forthright and Four-Square, he had ideals as high and as understandable as the mottoes on money. In the mind of America he *was* the army, the administration, the nation's shield and sword and stout right arm. His ideal was the American Dream.

"We are not fighting for money, for power, or for world domination," General Carpenter announced at the Press Association dinner.

"We are fighting solely for the American dream," he said to the 162nd Congress.

"Our aim is not aggression or the reduction of nations to slavery," he said at the West Point Annual Officer's Dinner.

"We are fighting for the Meaning of civilization," he told the San Francisco Pioneers' Club.

"We are struggling for the Ideal of civilization; for Culture, for Poetry, for the Only Things Worth Preserving," he said at the Chicago Wheat Pit Festival.

"This is a war for survival," he said. "We are not fighting for ourselves, but for our Dreams; for the Better Things in Life which must not disappear from the face of the earth."

America fought. General Carpenter asked for one hundred million men. The army was given one hundred million men. General Carpenter asked for ten thousand U-Bombs. Ten thousand U-Bombs were delivered and dropped. The enemy also dropped ten thousand U-Bombs and destroyed most of America's cities.

"We must dig in against the hordes of barbarism," General Carpenter said. "Give me a thousand engineers."

One thousand engineers were forthcoming, and a hun-

7

dred cities were dug and hollowed out beneath the rubble.

"Give me five hundred sanitation experts, eight hundred traffic managers, two hundred air-conditioning experts, one hundred city managers, one thousand communication chiefs, seven hundred personnel experts . . ."

The list of General Carpenter's demand for technical experts was endless. America did not know how to supply them.

"We must become a nation of experts," General Carpenter informed the National Association of American Universities. "Every man and woman must be a specific tool for a specific job, hardened and sharpened by your training and education to win the fight for the American Dream."

"Our Dream," General Carpenter said at the Wall Street Bond Drive Breakfast, "is at one with the gentle Greeks of Athens, with the noble Romans of . . . er . . . Rome. It is a dream of the Better Things in Life. Of Music and Art and Poetry and Culture. Money is only a weapon to be used in the fight for this dream. Ambition is only a ladder to climb to this dream. Ability is only a tool to shape this dream."

Wall Street applauded. General Carpenter asked for one hundred and fifty billion dollars, fifteen hundred dedicated dollar-a-year men, three thousand experts in mineralogy, petrology, mass production, chemical warfare and air-traffic time study. They were delivered. The country was in high gear. General Carpenter had only to press a button and an expert would be delivered.

In March of A.D. 2112 the war came to a climax and the American Dream was resolved, not on any one of the seven fronts where millions of men were locked in bitter combat, not in any of the staff headquarters or any of the capitals of the warring nations, not in any of the production centers spewing forth arms and supplies, but in Ward T of the United States Army Hospital buried three hundred feet below what had once been St. Albans, New York.

Ward T was something of a mystery at St. Albans. Like all army hospitals, St. Albans was organized with specific wards reserved for specific injuries. Right arm amputees were gathered in one ward; left arm amputees in another. Radiation burns, head injuries, eviscerations, secondary gamma poisonings and so on were each assigned their

specific location in the hospital organization. The Army
Medical Corps had established nineteen classes of combat
injury which included every possible kind of damage to
brain and tissue. These used up letters A to S. What,
then, was in Ward T?

No one knew. The doors were double locked. No visitors were permitted to enter. No patients were permitted
to leave. Physicians were seen to arrive and depart. Their
perplexed expressions stimulated the wildest speculations
but revealed nothing. The nurses who ministered to Ward
T were questioned eagerly but they were close-mouthed.

There were dribs and drabs of information, unsatis-
fying and self-contradictory. A charwoman asserted that
she had been in to clean up and there had been no one
in the ward. Absolutely no one. Just two dozen beds and
nothing else. Had the beds been slept in? Yes. They were
rumpled, some of them. Were there signs of the ward
being in use? Oh yes. Personal things on the tables and
so on. But dusty, kind of. Like they hadn't been used in a
long time.

Public opinion decided it was a ghost ward. For spooks
only.

But a night orderly reported passing the locked ward
and hearing singing from within. What kind of singing?
Foreign language, like. What language? The orderly
couldn't say. Some of the words sounded like . . . well,
like: Cow dee on us eager tour . . .

Public opinion started to run a fever and decided it
was an alien ward. For spies only.

St. Albans enlisted the help of the kitchen staff and
checked the food trays. Twenty-four trays went into
Ward T three times a day. Twenty-four came out. Sometimes the returning trays were emptied. Most times they
were untouched.

Public opinion built up pressure and decided that Ward
T was a racket. It was an informal club for goldbricks
and staff grafters who caroused within. Cow dee on us
eager tour indeed!

For gossip, a hospital can put a small town sewing
circle to shame with ease, but sick people are easily
goaded into passion by trivia. It took just three months
for idle speculation to turn into downright fury. In January, 2112, St. Albans was a sound, well-run hospital.
By March, 2112, St. Albans was in a ferment, and the
psychological unrest found its way into the official rec-

ords. The percentage of recoveries fell off. Malingering set in. Petty infractions increased. Mutinies flared. There was a staff shake-up. It did no good. Ward T was inciting the patients to riot. There was another shake-up, and another, and still the unrest fumed.

The news finally reached General Carpenter's desk through official channels.

"In our fight for the American Dream," he said, "we must not ignore those who have already given of themselves. Send me a Hospital Administration expert."

The expert was delivered. He could do nothing to heal St. Albans. General Carpenter read the reports and fired him.

"Pity," said General Carpenter, "is the first ingredient of civilization. Send me a Surgeon General."

A Surgeon General was delivered. He could not break the fury of St. Albans and General Carpenter broke him. But by this time Ward T was being mentioned in the dispatches.

"Send me," General Carpenter said, "the expert in charge of Ward T."

St. Albans sent a doctor, Captain Edsel Dimmock. He was a stout young man, already bald, only three years out of medical school but with a fine record as an expert in psychotherapy. General Carpenter liked experts. He liked Dimmock. Dimmock adored the general as the spokesman for a culture which he had been too specially trained to seek up to now, but which he hoped to enjoy after the war was won.

"Now look here, Dimmock," General Carpenter began. "We're all of us tools, today—hardened and sharpened to do a specific job. You know our motto: A job for everyone and everyone on the job. Somebody's not on the job at Ward T and we've got to kick him out. Now, in the first place what the hell is Ward T?"

Dimmock stuttered and fumbled. Finally he explained that it was a special ward set up for special combat cases. Shock cases.

"Then you do have patients in the ward?"

"Yes, sir. Ten women and fourteen men."

Carpenter brandished a sheaf of reports. "Says here the St. Albans patients claim nobody's in Ward T."

Dimmock was shocked. That was untrue, he assured the general.

"All right, Dimmock. So you've got your twenty-four

crocks in there. Their job's to get well. Your job's to cure them. What the hell's upsetting the hospital about that?"

"W-well, sir. Perhaps it's because we keep them locked up."

"You keep Ward T locked?"

"Yes, sir."

"Why?"

"To keep the patients in, General Carpenter."

"Keep 'em in? What d'you mean? Are they trying to get out? They violent, or something?"

"No, sir. Not violent."

"Dimmock, I don't like your attitude. You're acting damned sneaky and evasive. And I'll tell you something else I don't like. That T classification. I checked with a Filing Expert from the Medical Corps and there is no T classification. What the hell are you up to at St. Albans?"

"W-well, sir . . . We invented the T classification. It . . . They . . . They're rather special cases, sir. We don't know what to do about them or how to handle them. W-We've been trying to keep it quiet until we've worked out a modus operandi, but it's brand new, General Carpenter. Brand new!" Here the expert in Dimmock triumphed over discipline. "It's sensational. It'll make medical history, by God! It's the biggest damned thing ever."

"What is it, Dimmock? Be specific."

"Well, sir, they're shock cases. Blanked out. Almost cat-atonic. Very little respiration. Slow pulse. No response."

"I've seen thousands of shock cases like that," Carpenter grunted. "What's so unusual?"

"Yes, sir, so far it sounds like the standard Q or R classification. But here's something unusual. They don't eat and they don't sleep."

"Never?"

"Some of them never."

"Then why don't they die?"

"We don't know. The metabolism cycle's broken, but only on the anabolism side. Catabolism continues. In other words, sir, they're eliminating waste products but they're not taking anything in. They're eliminating fatigue poisons and rebuilding worn tissue, but without food and sleep. God knows how. It's fantastic."

"That why you've got them locked up? Mean to say . . . D'you suspect them of stealing food and cat naps somewhere else?"

"N-No, sir." Dimmock looked shamefaced. "I don't

know how to tell you this, General Carpenter. I . . . We
lock them up because of the real mystery. They . . . Well,
they disappear."

"They what?"

"They disappear, sir. Vanish. Right before your eyes."

"The hell you say."

"I do say, sir. They'll be sitting on a bed or standing
around. One minute you see them, the next minute you
don't. Sometimes there's two dozen in Ward T. Other times
none. They disappear and reappear without rhyme or
reason. That's why we've got the ward locked, General
Carpenter. In the entire history of combat and combat injury there's never been a case like this before. We don't
know how to handle it."

"Bring me three of those cases," General Carpenter said.

Nathan Riley ate French toast, eggs benedict; consumed two pints of brown ale, smoked a John Drew,
belched delicately and arose from the breakfast table.
He nodded quietly to Gentleman Jim Corbett, who
broke off his conversation with Diamond Jim Brady to
intercept him on the way to the cashier's desk.

"Who do you like for the pennant this year, Nat?" Gentleman Jim inquired.

"The Dodgers," Nathan Riley answered.

"They've got no pitching."

"They've got Snider and Furillo and Campanella. They'll
take the pennant this year, Jim. I'll bet they take it
earlier than any team ever did. By September 13. Make
a note. See if I'm right."

"You're always right, Nat," Corbett said.

Riley smiled, paid his check, sauntered out into the
street and caught a horsecar bound for Madison Square
Garden. He got off at the corner of Fiftieth Street and
Eighth Avenue and walked upstairs to a handbook office
over a radio repair shop. The bookie glanced at him,
produced an envelope and counted out fifteen thousand
dollars.

"Rocky Marciano by a TKO over Roland La Starza in
the eleventh," he said. "How the hell do you call them
so accurate, Nat?"

"That's the way I make a living," Riley smiled. "Are
you making book on the elections?"

"Eisenhower twelve to five. Stevenson—"

"Never mind Adlai." Riley placed twenty thousand dollars on the counter. "I'm backing Ike. Get this down for me."

He left the handbook office and went to his suite in the Waldorf where a tall, thin young man was waiting for him anxiously.

"Oh yes," Nathan Riley said. "You're Ford, aren't you? Harold Ford?"

"Henry Ford, Mr. Riley."

"And you need financing for that machine in your bicycle shop. What's it called?"

"I call it an Ipsimobile, Mr. Riley."

"Hmmm. Can't say I like that name. Why not call it an automobile?"

"That's a wonderful suggestion, Mr. Riley. I'll certainly take it."

"I like you, Henry. You're young, eager, adaptable. I believe in your future and I believe in your automobile. I'll invest two hundred thousand dollars in your company."

Riley wrote a check and ushered Henry Ford out. He glanced at his watch and suddenly felt impelled to go back and look around for a moment. He entered his bedroom, undressed, put on a gray shirt and gray slacks. Across the pocket of the shirt were large blue letters: U.S.A.H.

He locked the bedroom door and disappeared.

He reappeared in Ward T of the United States Army Hospital in St. Albans, standing alongside his bed which was one of twenty-four lining the walls of a long, light steel barracks. Before he could draw another breath, he was seized by three pairs of hands. Before he could struggle, he was shot by a pneumatic syringe and poleaxed by 1½ cc of sodium thiomorphate.

"We've got one," someone said.

"Hang around," someone else answered. "General Carpenter said he wanted three."

After Marcus Junius Brutus left her bed, Lela Machan clapped her hands. Her slave women entered the chamber and prepared her bath. She bathed, dressed, scented herself and breakfasted on Smyrna figs, Rose oranges and a flagon of Lachryma Christi. Then she smoked a cigarette and ordered her litter.

The gates of her house were crowded as usual by adoring hordes from the Twentieth Legion. Two centurions

removed her chair-bearers from the poles of the litter
and bore her on their stout shoulders. Lela Machan smiled.
A young man in a sapphire-blue cloak thrust through the
mob and ran toward her. A knife flashed in his hand.
Lela braced herself to meet death bravely.

"Lady!" he cried. "Lady Lela!"

He slashed his left arm with the knife and let the crimson blood stain her robe.

"This blood of mine is the least I have to give you," he
cried.

Lela touched his forehead gently.

"Silly boy," she murmured. "Why?"

"For love of you, my lady."

"You will be admitted tonight at nine," Lela whispered.
He stared at her until she laughed. "I promise you. What
is your name, pretty boy?"

"Ben Hur."

"Tonight at nine, Ben Hur."

The litter moved on. Outside the forum, Julius Caesar
passed in hot argument with Savanarola. When he saw
the litter he motioned sharply to the centurions, who
stopped at once. Caesar swept back the curtains and
stared at Lela, who regarded him languidly. Caesar's face
twitched.

"Why?" he asked hoarsely. "I have begged, pleaded, brib-
ed, wept, and all without forgiveness. Why, Lela? Why?"

"Do you remember Boadicea?" Lela murmured.

"Boadicea? Queen of the Britons? Good God, Lela,
what can she mean to our love? I did not love Boadicea.
I merely defeated her in battle."

"And killed her, Caesar."

"She poisoned herself, Lela."

"She was my mother, Caesar!" Suddenly Lela pointed
her finger at Caesar. "Murderer. You will be punished.
Beware the Ides of March, Caesar!"

Caesar recoiled in horror. The mob of admirers that
had gathered around Lela uttered a shout of approval.
Amidst a shower of rose petals and violets she continued
on her way across the Forum to the Temple of the Vestal
Virgins where she abandoned her adoring suitors and entered the sacred temple.

Before the altar she genuflected, intoned a prayer,
dropped a pinch of incense on the altar flame and dis-
robed. She examined her beautiful body reflected in a
silver mirror, then experienced a momentary twinge of

homesickness. She put on a gray blouse and a gray pair of slacks. Across the pocket of the blouse was lettered U.S.A.H.

She smiled once at the altar and disappeared.

She reappeared in Ward T of the United States Army Hospital where she was instantly felled by 1½ cc of sodium thiomorphate injected subcutaneously by a pneumatic syringe.

"That's two," somebody said.

"One more to go."

George Hanmer paused dramatically and stared around . . . at the opposition benches, at the Speaker on the woolsack, at the silver mace on a crimson cushion before the Speaker's chair. The entire House of Parliament, hypnotized by Hanmer's fiery oratory, waited breathlessly for him to continue.

"I can say no more," Hanmer said at last. His voice was choked with emotion. His face was blanched and grim. "I will fight for this bill at the beachheads. I will fight in the cities, the towns, the fields and the hamlets. I will fight for this bill to the death and, God willing, I will fight for it after death. Whether this be a challenge or a prayer, let the consciences of the right honorable gentlemen determine; but of one thing I am sure and determined: England must own the Suez Canal."

Hanmer sat down. The house exploded. Through the cheering and applause he made his way out into the division lobby where Gladstone, Churchill and Pitt stopped him to shake his hand. Lord Palmerston eyed him coldly, but Pam was shouldered aside by Disraeli who limped up, all enthusiasm, all admiration.

"We'll have a bite at Tattersall's," Dizzy said. "My car's waiting."

Lady Beaconfield was in the Rolls Royce outside the Houses of Parliament. She pinned a primrose on Dizzy's lapel and patted Hanmer's cheek affectionately.

"You've come a long way from the schoolboy who used to bully Dizzy, Georgie," she said.

Hanmer laughed. Dizzy sang: *"Gaudeamus igitur . . ."* and Hanmer chanted the ancient scholastic song until they reached Tattersall's. There Dizzy ordered Guinness and grilled bones while Hanmer went upstairs in the club to change.

For no reason at all he had the impulse to go back

for a last look. Perhaps he hated to break with his past completely. He divested himself of his surtout, nankeen waistcoat, pepper and salt trousers, polished Hessians and undergarments. He put on a gray shirt and gray trousers and disappeared.

He reappeared in Ward T of the St. Albans hospital where he was rendered unconscious by 1½ cc of sodium thiomorphate.

"That's three," somebody said.

"Take 'em to Carpenter."

So there they sat in General Carpenter's office, PFC Nathan Riley, M/Sgt Lela Machan, and Corp/2 George Hanmer. They were in their hospital grays. They were torpid with sodium thiomorphate.

The office had been cleared and it blazed with light. Present were experts from Espionage, Counter-Espionage, Security and Central Intelligence. When Captain Edsel Dimmock saw the steel-faced ruthless squad awaiting the patients and himself, he started. General Carpenter smiled grimly.

"Didn't occur to you that we mightn't buy your disappearance story, eh Dimmock?"

"S-Sir?"

"I'm an expert too, Dimmock. I'll spell it out for you. The war's going badly. Very badly. There've been intelligence leaks. The St. Albans mess might point to you."

"B-But they do disappear, sir. I—"

"My experts want to talk to you and your patients about this disappearing act, Dimmock. They'll start with you."

The experts worked over Dimmock with preconscious softeners, id releases and superego blocks. They tried every truth serum in the books and every form of physical and mental pressure. They brought Dimmock, squealing, to the breaking point three times, but there was nothing to break.

"Let him stew for now," Carpenter said. "Get on to the patients."

The experts appeared reluctant to apply pressure to the sick men and the woman.

"For God's sake, don't be squeamish," Carpenter raged. "We're fighting a war for civilization. We've got to protect our ideals no matter what the price. Get to it!"

The experts from Espionage, Counter-Espionage, Security and Central Intelligence got to it. Like three candles, PFC Nathan Riley, M/Sgt Lela Machan and Corp/2 George Hanmer snuffed out and disappeared. One moment they were seated in chairs surrounded by violence. The next moment they were not.

The experts gasped. General Carpenter did the handsome thing. He stalked to Dimmock. "Captain Dimmock, I apologize. Colonel Dimmock, you've been promoted for making an important discovery . . . only what the hell does it mean? We've got to check ourselves first."

Carpenter snapped up the intercom. "Get me a combat-shock expert and an alienist."

The two experts entered and were briefed. They examined the witnesses. They considered.

"You're all suffering from a mild case of shock," the combat-shock expert said. "War jitters."

"You mean we didn't see them disappear?"

The shock expert shook his head and glanced at the alienist who also shook his head.

"Mass illusion," the alienist said.

At that moment PFC Riley, M/Sgt Machan and Corp/2 Hanmer reappeared. One moment they were a mass illusion; the next, they were back sitting in their chairs surrounded by confusion.

"Dope 'em again, Dimmock," Carpenter cried. "Give 'em a gallon." He snapped up his intercom. "I want every expert we've got. Emergency meeting in my office at once."

Thirty-seven experts, hardened and sharpened tools all, inspected the unconscious shock cases and discussed them for three hours. Certain facts were obvious: This must be a new fantastic syndrome brought on by the new and fantastic horrors of the war. As combat technique develops, the response of victims of this technique must also take new roads. For every action there is an equal and opposite reaction. Agreed.

This new syndrome must involve some aspects of teleportation . . . the power of mind over space. Evidently combat shock, while destroying certain known powers of the mind must develop other latent powers hitherto unknown. Agreed.

Obviously, the patients must only be able to return to the point of departure, otherwise they would not continue to return to Ward T nor would they have returned to General Carpenter's office. Agreed.

Obviously, the patients must be able to procure food and sleep wherever they go, since neither was required in Ward T. Agreed.

"One small point," Colonel Dimmock said. "They seem to be returning to Ward T less frequently. In the beginning they would come and go every day or so. Now most of them stay away for weeks and hardly ever return."

"Never mind that," Carpenter said. "Where do they go?"

"Do they teleport behind the enemy lines?" someone asked. "There's those intelligence leaks."

"I want Intelligence to check," Carpenter snapped. "Is the enemy having similar difficulties with, say, prisoners of war who appear and disappear from their POW camps? They might be some of ours from Ward T."

"They might simply be going home," Colonel Dimmock suggested.

"I want Security to check," Carpenter ordered. "Cover the home life and associations of every one of those twenty-four disappearers. Now . . . about our operations in Ward T. Colonel Dimmock has a plan."

"We'll set up six extra beds in Ward T," Edsel Dimmock explained. "We'll send in six experts to live there and observe. Information must be picked up indirectly from the patients. They're catatonic and nonresponsive when conscious, and incapable of answering questions when drugged."

"Gentlemen," Carpenter summed it up. "This is the greatest potential weapon in the history of warfare. I don't have to tell you what it can mean to us to be able to teleport an entire army behind enemy lines. We can win the war for the American Dream in one day if we can win this secret hidden in those shattered minds. We must win!"

The experts hustled, Security checked, Intelligence probed. Six hardened and sharpened tools moved into Ward T in St. Albans Hospital and slowly got acquainted with the disappearing patients who reappeared less and less frequently. The tension increased.

Security was able to report that not one case of strange appearance had taken place in America in the past year. Intelligence reported that the enemy did not seem to be having similiar difficulties with their own shock cases or with POWs.

Carpenter fretted. "This is all brand new. We've got no

specialists to handle it. We've got to develop new tools."
He snapped up his intercom. "Get me a college," he said.

They got him Yale.

"I want some experts in mind over matter. Develop
them," Carpenter ordered. Yale at once introduced three
graduate courses in Thaumaturgy, Extrasensory Percep-
tion and Telekinesis.

The first break came when one of the Ward T experts
requested the assistance of another expert. He needed a
Lapidary.

"What the hell for?" Carpenter wanted to know.

"He picked up a reference to a gem stone," Colonel
Dimmock explained. "He's a personnel specialist and he
can't relate it to anything in his experience."

"And he's not supposed to," Carpenter said approving-
ly. "A job for every man and every man on the job." He
flipped up the intercom. "Get me a Lapidary."

An expert Lapidary was given leave of absence from the
army arsenal and asked to identify a type of diamond
called Jim Brady. He could not.

"We'll try it from another angle," Carpenter said. He
snapped up his intercom. "Get me a Semanticist."

The Semanticist left his desk in the War Propaganda Department but could make nothing of the words Jim Brady.
They were names to him. No more. He suggested a Genealogist.

A Genealogist was given one day's leave from his post
with the Un-American Ancestors Committee but could
make nothing of the name Brady beyond the fact that it
had been a common name in America for five hundred
years. He suggested an Archaeologist.

An Archaeologist was released from the Cartography
Division of Invasion Command and instantly identified
the name Diamond Jim Brady. It was a historic person-
age who had been famous in the city of Little Old New
York some time between Governor Peter Stuyvesant and
Governor Fiorello La Guardia.

"Christ!" Carpenter marveled. "That's ages ago. Where
the hell did Nathan Riley get that? You'd better join the
experts in Ward T and follow this up."

The Archaeologist followed it up, checked his references and sent in his report. Carpenter read it and was
stunned. He called an emergency meeting of his staff of
experts.

"Gentlemen," he announced, "Ward T is something big-

ger than teleportation. Those shock patients are doing
something far more incredible . . . far more meaningful.
Gentlemen, they're traveling through time."

The staff rustled uncertainly. Carpenter nodded emphatically.

"Yes, gentlemen. Time travel is here. It has not arrived the way we expected it . . . as a result of expert
research by qualified specialists; it has come as a plague
. . . an infection . . . a disease of the war . . . a result of
combat injury to ordinary men. Before I continue, look
through these reports for documentation."

The staff read the stenciled sheets. PFC Nathan Riley
. . . disappearing into the early twentieth century in New
York; M/Sgt Lela Machan . . . visiting the first century
in Rome; Corp/2 George Hanmer . . . journeying into the
nineteenth century in England. And all the rest of the
twenty-four patients, escaping the turmoil and horrors of
modern war in the twenty-second century by fleeing to
Venice and the Doges, to Jamaica and the buccaneers, to
China and the Han Dynasty, to Norway and Eric the
Red, to any place and any time in the world.

"I needn't point out the colossal significance of this discovery," General Carpenter pointed out. "Think what it
would mean to the war if we could send an army back
in time a week or a month or a year. We could win the
war before it started. We could protect our Dream . . .
Poetry and Beauty and the Culture of America . . . from
barbarism without ever endangering it."

The staff tried to grapple with the problem of winning
battles before they started.

"The situation is complicated by the fact that these
men and women of Ward T are *non compos*. They may
or may not know how they do what they do, but in any
case they're incapable of communicating with the experts who could reduce this miracle to method. It's for
us to find the key. They can't help us."

The hardened and sharpened specialists looked around
uncertainly.

"We'll need experts," General Carpenter said.

The staff relaxed. They were on familiar ground again.

"We'll need a Cerebral Mechanist, a Cyberneticist, a
Psychiatrist, an Anatomist, an Archaeologist and a first-
rate Historian. They'll go into that ward and they won't
come out until their job is done. They must learn the
technique of time travel."

The first five experts were easy to draft from other war departments. All America was a tool chest of hardened and sharpened specialists. But there was trouble locating a first-class Historian until the Federal Penitentiary co-operated with the army and released Dr. Bradley Scrim from his twenty years at hard labor. Dr. Scrim was acid and jagged. He had held the chair of Philosophic History at a Western university until he spoke his mind about the war for the American Dream. That got him the twenty years hard.

Scrim was still intransigent, but induced to play ball by the intriguing problem of Ward T.

"But I'm not an expert," he snapped. "In this be-nighted nation of experts, I'm the last singing grasshopper in the ant heap."

Carpenter snapped up the intercom. "Get me an En-tomologist," he said.

"Don't bother," Scrim said. "I'll translate. You're a nest of ants . . . all working and toiling and specializing. For what?"

"To preserve the American Dream," Carpenter an-swered hotly. "We're fighting for Poetry and Culture and Education and the Finer Things in Life."

"Which means you're fighting to preserve me," Scrim said. "That's what I've devoted my life to. And what do you do with me? Put me in jail."

"You were convicted of enemy sympathizing and fellow-travelling," Carpenter said.

"I was convicted of believing in *my* American Dream," Scrim said. "Which is another way of saying I was jailed for having a mind of my own."

Scrim was also intransigent in Ward T. He stayed one night, enjoyed three good meals, read the reports, threw them down and began hollering to be let out.

"There's a job for everyone and everyone must be on the job," Colonel Dimmock told him. "You don't come out until you've got the secret of time travel."

"There's no secret I can get," Scrim said.

"Do they travel in time?"

"Yes and no."

"The answer has to be one or the other. Not both. You're evading the—"

"Look," Scrim interrupted wearily. "What are you an expert in?"

"Psychotherapy."

"Then how the hell can you understand what I'm talking about? This is a philosophic concept. I tell you there's no secret here that the army can use. There's no secret any group can use. It's a secret for individuals only."

"I don't understand you."

"I didn't think you would. Take me to Carpenter."

They took Scrim to Carpenter's office where he grinned at the general malignantly, looking for all the world like a redheaded, underfed devil.

"I'll need ten minutes," Scrim said. "Can you spare them out of your tool box?"

Carpenter nodded.

"Now listen carefully. I'm going to give you the clues to something so vast and so strange that it will need all your fine edge to cut into it."

Carpenter looked expectant.

"Nathan Riley goes back in time to the early twentieth century. There he lives the life of his fondest dreams. He's a big-time gambler, the friend of Diamond Jim Brady and others. He wins money betting on events because he always knows the outcome in advance. He won money betting on Eisenhower to win an election. He won money betting on a prize fighter named Marciano to beat another prize fighter named La Starza. He made money investing in an automobile company owned by Henry Ford. There are the clues. They mean anything to you?"

"Not without a Sociological Analyst," Carpenter answered. He reached for the intercom.

"Don't order one, I'll explain later. Let's try some more clues. Lela Machan, for example. She escapes into the Roman Empire where she lives the life of her dreams as a *femme fatale*. Every man loves her. Julius Caesar, Savonarola, the entire Twentieth Legion, a man named Ben Hur. Do you see the fallacy?"

"No."

"She also smokes cigarettes."

"Well?" Carpenter asked after a pause.

"I continue," Scrim said. "George Hanmer escapes into England of the nineteenth century where he's a member of Parliament and the friend of Gladstone, Winston Churchill and Disraeli, who takes him riding in his Rolls Royce. Do you know what a Rolls Royce is?"

"No."

"It was the name of an automobile."

"So?"

"You don't understand yet?"

"No."

Scrim paced the floor in exaltation. "Carpenter, this is a bigger discovery than teleportation or time travel. This can be the salvation of man. I don't think I'm exaggerating. Those two dozen shock victims in Ward T have been H-Bombed into something so gigantic that it's no wonder your specialists and experts can't understand it."

"What the hell's bigger than time travel, Scrim?"

"Listen to this, Carpenter. Eisenhower did not run for office until the middle of the twentieth century. Nathan Riley could not have been a friend of Diamond Jim Brady's and bet on Eisenhower to win an election . . . not simultaneously. Brady was dead a quarter of a century before Ike was President. Marciano defeated La Starza fifty years after Henry Ford started his automobile company. Nathan Riley's time traveling is full of similar anachronisms."

Carpenter looked puzzled.

"Lela Machan could not have had Ben Hur for a lover. Ben Hur never existed in Rome. He never existed at all. He was a character in a novel. She couldn't have smoked. They didn't have tobacco then. You see? More anachronisms. Disraeli could never have taken George Hanmer for a ride in a Rolls Royce because automobiles weren't invented until long after Disraeli's death."

"The hell you say," Carpenter exclaimed. "You mean they're all lying?"

"No. Don't forget, they don't need sleep. They don't need food. They're not lying. They're going back in time all right. They're eating and sleeping back there."

"But you just said their stories don't stand up. They're full of anachronisms."

"Because they travel back into a time of their own imagination. Nathan Riley has his own picture of what America was like in the early twentieth century. It's faulty and anachronistic because he's no scholar, but it's real for him. He can live there. The same is true for the others."

Carpenter goggled.

"The concept is almost beyond understanding. These people have discovered how to turn dreams into reality. They know how to enter their dream realities. They can stay there, live there, perhaps forever. My God, Carpenter, *this* is your American dream. It's miracle-working, immortality, Godlike creation, mind over matter . . . It must be explored. It must be studied. It must be given to the world."

"Can you do it, Scrim?"

"No, I cannot. I'm an historian. I'm noncreative, so it's beyond me. You need a poet . . . an artist who understands the creation of dreams. From creating dreams on paper it oughtn't to be too difficult to take the step to creating dreams in actuality."

"A poet? Are you serious?"

"Certainly I'm serious. Don't you know what a poet is? You've been telling us for five years that this war is being fought to save the poets."

"Don't be facetious, Scrim, I—"

"Send a poet into Ward T. He'll learn how they do it. He's the only man who can. A poet is half doing it anyway. Once he learns, he can teach your psychologists and anatomists. Then they can teach us; but the poet is the only man who can interpret between those shock cases and your experts."

"I believe you're right, Scrim."

"Then don't delay, Carpenter. Those patients are returning to this world less and less frequently. We've got to get at that secret before they disappear forever. Send a poet to Ward T."

Carpenter snapped up his intercom. "Send me a poet," he said.

He waited, and waited . . . and waited . . . while America sorted feverishly through its two hundred and ninety millions of hardened and sharpened experts, its specialized tools to defend the American Dream of Beauty and Poetry and the Better Things in Life. He waited for them to find a poet, not understanding the endless delay, the fruitless search; not understanding why Bradley Scrim laughed and laughed and laughed at this final, fatal disappearance.

*

Adam and No Eve

KRANE KNEW THIS MUST BE THE SEACOAST. INSTINCT told him; but more than instinct, the few shreds of knowl-

edge that clung to his torn brain told him; the stars that
had shown at night through the rare breaks in the clouds,
and his compass that still pointed a trembling finger north.
That was strangest of all, Krane thought. The rubbled
Earth still retained its polarity.

It was no longer a coast; there was no longer any sea.
Only the faint line of what had been a cliff stretched
north and south for endless miles. It was a line of gray
ash; the same gray ash and cinders that lay behind him
and stretched before him. . . . Fine silt, knee-deep, that
swirled up at every motion and choked him; cinders that
scudded in dense night clouds when the mad winds blew;
black dust that was churned to mud when the frequent
rains fell.

The sky was jet overhead. The heavy clouds rode
high and were pierced with shafts of sunlight that marched
swiftly over the Earth. Where the light struck a cinder
storm, it was filled with gusts of dancing, gleaming particles. Where it played through rain it brought the arches
of rainbows into being. Rain fell; cinder-storms blew;
light thrust down—together, alternately and continually
in a jigsaw of black and white violence. So it had been
for months. So it was over every mile of the broad Earth.

Krane passed the edge of the ashen cliffs and began
crawling down the even slope that had once been the
ocean bed. He had been traveling so long that pain had
become part of him. He braced elbows and dragged his
body forward. Then he brought his right knee under him
and reached forward with elbows again. Elbows, knee,
elbows, knee—He had forgotten what it was to walk.

Life, he thought dazedly, is miraculous. It adapts itself to anything. If it must crawl, it crawls. Callous forms
on the elbows and knees. The neck and shoulders tough-
en. The nostrils learn to snort away the ashes before they
breathe. The bad leg swells and festers. It numbs, and
presently it will rot and fall off.

"I beg pardon?" Krane said, "I didn't quite get that—"

He peered up at the tall figure before him and tried to
understand the words. It was Hallmyer. He wore his
stained lab coat and his gray hair was awry. Hallmyer
stood delicately on top of the ashes and Krane wondered
why he could see the scudding cinder clouds through his
body.

"How do you like your world, Steven?" Hallmyer asked.
Krane shook his head miserably.

"Not very pretty, eh?" said Hallmyer. "Look around you. Dust, that's all; dust and ashes. Crawl, Steven, crawl. You'll find nothing but dust and ashes—"

Hallmyer produced a goblet of water from nowhere. It was clear and cold. Krane could see the fine mist of dew on its surface and his mouth was suddenly coated with grit.

"Hallmyer!" he cried. He tried to get to his feet and reach for the water, but the jolt of pain in his right leg warned him. He crouched back.

Hallmyer sipped and then spat in his face. The water felt warm.

"Keep crawling," said Hallmyer bitterly. "Crawl round and round the face of the Earth. You'll find nothing but dust and ashes—" He emptied the goblet on the ground before Krane. "Keep crawling. How many miles? Figure it out for yourself. Pi-times D. The diameter is eight thousand or so—"

He was gone, coat and goblet. Krane realized that rain was falling again. He pressed his face into the warm cinder mud, opened his mouth and tried to suck the moisture. Presently he began crawling again.

There was an instinct that drove him on. He had to get somewhere. It was associated, he knew, with the sea—with the edge of the sea. At the shore of the sea something waited for him. Something that would help him understand all this. He had to get to the sea—that is, if there was a sea any more.

The thundering rain beat his back like heavy planks. Krane paused and yanked the knapsack around to his side where he probed in it with one hand. It contained exactly three things. A gun, a bar of chocolate and a can of peaches. All that was left of two months' supplies. The chocolate was pulpy and spoiled. Krane knew he had best eat it before all value rotted away. But in another day he would lack the strength to open the can. He pulled it out and attacked it with the opener. By the time he had pierced and pried away a flap of tin, the rain had passed.

As he munched the fruit and sipped the juice, he watched the wall of rain marching before him down the slope of the ocean bed. Torrents of water were gushing through the mud. Small channels had already been cut— channels that would be new rivers some day; a day he would never see; a day that no living thing would ever see. As he flipped the empty can aside, Krane thought: The last living thing on Earth eats its last meal. Metabolism begins the last act.

Wind would follow the rain. In the endless weeks that he had been crawling, he had learned that. Wind would come in a few minutes and flog him with its clouds of cinders and ashes. He crawled forward, bleary eyes searching the flat gray miles for cover.

Evelyn tapped his shoulder.

Krane knew it was she before he turned his head. She stood alongside, fresh and gay in her bright dress, but her lovely face was puckered with alarm.

"Steven," she said, "you've got to hurry!"

He could only admire the way her smooth hair waved to her shoulders.

"Oh, darling!" she said, "you've been hurt!" Her quick gentle hands touched his legs and back. Krane nodded.

"Got it landing," he said. "I wasn't used to a parachute. I always thought you came down gently—like plumping onto a bed. But the earth came up at me like a fist—And Umber was fighting around in my arms. I couldn't let him drop, could I?"

"Of course not, dear," Evelyn said.

"So I just held on to him and tried to get my legs under me," Krane said. "And then something smashed my legs and side—"

He hesitated, wondering how much she knew of what really had happened. He didn't want to frighten her.

"Evelyn, darling—" he said, trying to reach up his arms.

"No dear," she said. She looked back in fright. "You've got to hurry. You've got to watch out behind!"

"The cinder storms?" He grimaced. "I've been through them before."

"Not the storms!" Evelyn cried. "Something else. Oh, Steven—"

Then she was gone, but Krane knew she had spoken the truth. There was something behind—something that had been following him. In the back of his mind he had sensed the menace. It was closing in on him like a shroud. He shook his head. Somehow that was impossible. He was the last living thing on Earth. How could there be a menace?

The wind roared behind him, and an instant later came the heavy clouds of cinders and ashes. They lashed over

him, biting his skin. With dimming eyes, he saw the way
they coated the mud and covered it with a fine dry
carpet. Krane drew his knees under him and covered his
head with his arms. With the knapsack as a pillow, he
prepared to wait out the storm. It would pass as quickly
as the rain.

The storm whipped up a great bewilderment in his
sick head. Like a child he pushed at the pieces of his
memory, trying to fit them together. Why was Hallmyer
so bitter toward him? It couldn't have been that argument, could it?

What argument?

Why, that one before all this happened.

Oh, that!

Abruptly, the pieces locked together.

Krane stood alongside the sleek lines of his ship and
admired it tremendously. The roof of the shed had been
removed and the nose of the ship hoisted so that it rested
on a cradle pointed toward the sky. A workman was
carefully burnishing the inner surfaces of the rocket jets.

The muffled sounds of swearing came from within the
ship and then a heavy clanking. Krane ran up the short
iron ladder to the port and thrust his head inside. A few
feet beneath him, two men were clamping the long tanks
of ferrous solution into place.

"Easy there," Krane called. "Want to knock the ship
apart?"

One looked up and grinned. Krane knew what he was
thinking. That the ship would tear itself apart. Everyone
said that. Everyone except Evelyn. She had faith in him.
Hallmyer never said it either, but Hallmyer thought he
was crazy in another way. As he descended the ladder,
Krane saw Hallmyer come into the shed, lab coat flying.

"Speak of the devil!" Krane muttered.

Hallmyer began shouting as soon as he saw Krane.
"Now listen—"

"Not all over again," Krane said.

Hallmyer dug a sheaf of papers out of his pocket and
waved it under Krane's nose.

"I've been up half the night," he said, "working it
through again. I tell you I'm right. I'm absolutely right—"

Krane looked at the tight-written equations and then
at Hallmyer's bloodshot eyes. The man was half mad
with fear.

"For the last time," Hallmyer went on. "You're using your new catalyst on iron solution. All right. I grant that it's a miraculous discovery. I give you credit for that."

Miraculous was hardly the word for it. Krane knew that without conceit, for he realized he'd only stumbled on it. You had to stumble on a catalyst that would induce atomic disintegration of iron and give 10×10^{10} foot-pounds of energy for every gram of fuel. No man was smart enough to think all that up by himself.

"You don't think I'll make it?" Krane asked.

"To the Moon? Around the Moon? Maybe. You've got a fifty-fifty chance." Hallmyer ran fingers through his lank hair. "But for God's sake, Steven, I'm not worried about you. If you want to kill yourself, that's your own affair. It's the Earth I'm worried about——"

"Nonsense. Go home and sleep it off."

"Look——" Hallmyer pointed to the sheets of paper with a shaky hand——"No matter how you work the feed and mixing system you can't get 100 per cent efficiency in the mixing and discharge."

"That's what makes it a fifty-fifty chance," Krane said. "So what's bothering you?"

"The catalyst that will escape through the rocket tubes. Do you realize what it'll do if a drop hits the Earth? It'll start a chain of disintegration that'll envelop the globe. It'll reach out to every iron atom——and there's iron everywhere. There won't be any Earth left for you to return to——"

"Listen," Krane said wearily, "we've been through all this before."

He took Hallmyer to the base of the rocket cradle. Beneath the iron framework was a two-hundred-foot pit, fifty feet wide and lined with firebrick.

"That's for the initial discharge flames. If any of the catalyst goes through, it'll be trapped in this pit and taken care of by the secondary reactions. Satisfied now?"

"But while you're in flight," Hallmyer persisted, "you'll be endangering the Earth until you're beyond Roche's limit. Every drop of non-activated catalyst will eventually sink back to the ground and——"

"For the very last time," Krane said grimly, "the flame of the rocket discharge takes care of that. It will envelop any escaped particles and destroy them. Now get out. I've got work to do."

As Krane pushed him to the door, Hallmyer screamed

and waved his arms. "I won't let you do it!" he repeated
over and over. "I won't let you risk it—"

Work? No, it was sheer intoxication to labor over the
ship. It had the fine beauty of a well-made thing. The
beauty of polished armor, of a balanced swept-hilt rapier,
of a pair of matched guns. There was no thought of
danger and death in Krane's mind as he wiped his hands
with waste after the last touches were finished.

She lay in the cradle ready to pierce the skies. Fifty
feet of slender steel, the rivet heads gleaming like jewels.
Thirty feet were given over to fuel and catalyst. Most of
the forward compartment contained the spring hammock
Krane had devised to absorb the acceleration strain. The
ship's nose was a porthole of natural crystal that stared
upward like a cyclopian eye.

Krane thought: She'll die after this trip. She'll return to
the Earth and smash in a blaze of fire and thunder, for
there's no way yet of devising a safe landing for a rocket
ship. But it's worth it. She'll have had her one great
flight, and that's all any of us should want. One great
beautiful flight into the unknown—

As he locked the workshop door, Krane heard Hallmyer shouting from the cottage across the fields. Through
the evening gloom he could see him waving urgently. He
trotted through the crisp stubble, breathing the sharp air
deeply, grateful to be alive.

"It's Evelyn on the phone," Hallmyer said.

Krane stared at him. Hallmyer refused to meet his eyes.

"What's the idea?" Krane asked. "I thought we agreed
that she wasn't to call—wasn't to get in touch with me
until I was ready to start? You been putting ideas into her
head? Is this the way you're going to stop me?"

Hallmyer said: "No—" and studiously examined the
darkening horizon.

Krane went into his study and picked up the phone.

"Now listen, darling," he said without preamble,
"there's no sense getting alarmed now. I explained everything very carefully. Just before the ship crashes, I take
to a parachute. I love you very much and I'll see you
Wednesday when I start. So long—"

"Good-by, sweetheart," Evelyn's clear voice said, "and
is that what you called me for?"

"Called you!"

A brown hulk disengaged itself from the hearth rug

and lifted itself to strong legs. Umber, Krane's mastiff, sniffed and cocked an ear. Then he whined.

"Did you say I called you?" Krane repeated.

Umber's throat suddenly poured forth a bellow. He reached Krane in a single bound, looked up into his face and whined and roared all at once.

"Shut up, you monster!" Krane said. He pushed Umber away with his foot.

"Give Umber a kick for me," Evelyn laughed. "Yes, dear. Someone called and said you wanted to speak to me."

"They did, eh? Look, honey, I'll call you back—"

Krane hung up. He arose doubtfully and watched Umber's uneasy actions. Through the windows, the late evening glow sent flickering shadows of orange light. Umber gazed at the light, sniffed and bellowed again. Suddenly struck, Krane leaped to the window.

Across the fields a mass of flame thrust high into the air, and within it was the crumbling walls of the workshop. Silhouetted against the blaze, the figures of half a dozen men darted and ran.

Krane shot out of the cottage and with Umber hard at his heels, sprinted toward the shed. As he ran he could see the graceful nose of the spaceship within the fire, still looking cool and untouched. If only he could reach it before the flames softened its metal and started the rivets.

The workmen trotted up to him, grimy and panting. Krane gaped at them in a mixture of fury and bewilderment.

"Hallmyer!" he shouted. "Hallmyer!"

Hallmyer pushed through the crowd. His eyes gleamed with triumph.

"Too bad," he said. "I'm sorry, Steven—"

"You bastard!" Krane shouted. He grasped Hallmyer by the lapels and shook him once. Then he dropped him and started into the shed.

Hallmyer snapped orders to the workmen and an instant later a body hurtled against Krane's calves and spilled him to the ground. He lurched to his feet, fists swinging. Umber was alongside, growling over the roar of the flames. Krane battered a man in the face, and saw him stagger back against a second. He lifted a knee in a vicious drive that sent the last workman crumpling to the ground. Then he ducked his head and plunged into the shop.

The scorch felt cool at first, but when he reached the
ladder and began mounting to the port, he screamed
with the agony of his burns. Umber was howling at the
foot of the ladder, and Krane realized that the dog could
never escape from the rocket blasts. He reached down
and hauled Umber into the ship.

Krane was reeling as he closed and locked the port.
He retained consciousness barely long enough to settle
himself in the spring hammock. Then instinct alone
prompted his hands to reach out toward the control
board; instinct and the frenzied refusal to let his beautiful ship waste itself in the flames. He would fail—yes.
But he would fail trying.

His fingers tripped the switches. The ship shuddered
and roared. And blackness descended over him.

How long was he unconscious? There was no telling.
Krane awoke with cold pressing against his face and
body, and the sound of frightened yelps in his ears.
Krane looked up and saw Umber tangled in the springs
and straps of the hammock. His first impulse was to
laugh, then suddenly he realized; he had looked *up!*
He had looked up at the hammock.

He was lying curled in the cup of the crystal nose.
The ship had risen high—perhaps almost to Roche's zone,
to the limit of the Earth's gravitational attraction, but then
without guiding hands at the controls to continue its
flight, had turned and was dropping back toward Earth.
Krane peered through the crystal and gasped.

Below him was the ball of the Earth. It looked three
times the size of the Moon. And it was no longer his
Earth. It was a globe of fire mottled with black clouds.
At the northernmost pole there was a tiny patch of
white, and even as Krane watched, it was suddenly
blotted over with hazy tones of red, scarlet and crimson.
Hallmyer had been right.

Krane lay frozen in the cup of the nose as the ship
descended, watching the flames gradually fade away to
leave nothing but the dense blanket of black around the
Earth. He lay numb with horror, unable to understand—
unable to reckon up a people snuffed out, a green fair
planet reduced to ashes and cinders. Everything that was
once dear and close to him—gone. He could not think of
Evelyn.

Air, whistling outside, awoke some instinct in him.

The few shreds of reason left told him to go down with his ship and forget everything in the thunder and destruction, but the instinct of life forced him to action. He climbed up to the store chest and prepared for the landing. Parachute, a small oxygen tank—a knapsack of supplies. Only half aware of what he was doing he dressed for the descent, buckled on the 'chute and opened the port. Umber whined pathetically, and he took the heavy dog in his arms and stepped out into space.

But space hadn't been so clogged, the way it was now. Then it had been difficult to breathe. But that was because the air had been rare—not filled with clogging grit like now.

Every breath was a lungful of ground glass—or ashes—or cinders—He had returned to a suffocating black present that hugged him with soft weight and made him fight for breath. Krane struggled in panic, and then relaxed.

It had happened before. A long time past he'd been buried deep under ashes when he'd stopped to remember. Weeks ago—or days—or months. Krane clawed with his hands, inching out of the mound of cinders that the wind had thrown over him. Presently he emerged into the light again. The wind had died away. It was time to begin his crawl to the sea once more.

The vivid pictures of his memory scattered again before the grim vista that stretched out ahead. Krane scowled. He remembered too much, and too often. He had the vague hope that if he remembered hard enough, he might change one of the things he had done—just a very little thing—and then all this would become untrue. He thought: It might help if everyone remembered and wished at the same time—but there isn't any everyone. I'm the only one. I'm the last memory on Earth. I'm the last life.

He crawled. Elbows, knee, elbows, knee—And then Hallmyer was crawling alongside and making a great game of it. He chortled and plunged in the cinders like a happy sea lion.

Krane said: "But why do we have to get to the sea?"

Hallmyer blew a spume of ashes.

"Ask her," he said, pointing to Krane's other side.

Evelyn was there, crawling seriously, intently, mimicking Krane's smallest action.

"It's because of our house," she said. "You remember

our house, darling? High on the cliff. We were going to
live there forever and ever. I was there when you left.
Now you're coming back to the house at the edge of the
sea. Your beautiful flight is over, dear, and you're coming back to me. We'll live together, just we two, like Adam
and Eve——"

Krane said: "That's nice."

Then Evelyn turned her head and screamed: "Oh,
Steven! Watch out!" and Krane felt the menace closing in
on him again. Still crawling, he stared back at the vast
gray plains of ash, and saw nothing. When he looked at
Evelyn again he saw only his shadow, sharp and black.
Presently, it too, faded away as the marching shaft of
sunlight passed.

But the dread remained. Evelyn had warned him twice,
and she was always right. Krane stopped and turned,
and settled himself to watch. If he was really being followed, he would see whatever it was, coming along his
tracks.

There was a painful moment of lucidity. It cleaved
through his fever and bewilderment, bringing with it the
sharpness and strength of a knife.

I'm mad, he thought. The corruption in my leg has
spread to my brain. There is no Evelyn, no Hallmyer,
no menace. In all this land there is no life but mine—
and even ghosts and spirits of the underworld must have
perished in the inferno that girdled the planet. No—
there is nothing but me and my sickness. I'm dying—
and when I perish, everything will perish. Only a mass
of lifeless cinders will go on.

But there was a movement.

Instinct again—Krane dropped his head and lay still.
Through slitted eyes he watched the ashen plains, wondering if death was playing tricks with his eyes. Another
façade of rain was beating down toward him, and he
hoped he could make sure before all vision was obliterated.

Yes. There.

A quarter mile back, a gray-brown shape was flitting
along the gray surface. Despite the drone of the distant
rain, Krane could hear the whisper of trodden cinders
and see the little clouds kicking up. Stealthily he groped
for the revolver in the knapsack as his mind reached
feebly for explanations and recoiled from fear.

The thing approached, and suddenly Krane squinted and understood. He recalled Umber kicking with fear and springing away from him when the 'chute landed them on the ashen face of the Earth.

"Why, it's Umber," he murmured. He raised himself. The dog halted. "Here, boy!" Krane croaked gaily. "Here, boy!"

He was overcome with joy. He realized that loneliness had hung over him, a horrible sensation of oneness in emptiness. Now his was not the only life. There was another. A friendly life that could offer love and companionship. Hope kindled again.

"Here, boy!" he repeated. "Come on, boy—"

After a while he stopped trying to snap his fingers. The Mastiff hung back, showing fangs and a lolling tongue. The dog was emaciated and its eyes gleamed red in the dusk. As Krane called once more, the dog snarled. Puffs of ash leaped beneath its nostrils.

He's hungry, Krane thought, that's all. He reached into the knapsack and at the gesture the dog snarled again. Krane withdrew the chocolate bar and laboriously peeled off the paper and silver foil. Weakly he tossed it toward Umber. It fell far short. After a minute of savage uncertainty, the dog advanced slowly and snapped up the food. Ashes powdered its muzzle. It licked its chops ceaselessly and continued to advance on Krane.

Panic jerked within him. A voice persisted: This is no friend. He has no love or companionship for you. Love and companionship have vanished from the land along with life. Now there is nothing left but hunger.

"No—" Krane whispered. "That isn't right that we should tear at each other and seek to devour—"

But Umber was advancing with a slinking sidle, and his teeth showed sharp and white. And even as Krane stared at him, the dog snarled and lunged.

Krane thrust up an arm under the dog's muzzle, but the weight of the charge carried him backward. He cried out in agony as his broken, swollen leg was struck by the weight of the dog. With his free hand he struck weakly, again and again, scarcely feeling the grind of teeth on his left arm. Then something metallic was pressed under him and he realized he was lying on the revolver he had let fall.

He groped for it and prayed the cinders had not clogged it. As Umber let go his arm and tore at his throat, Krane brought the gun up and jabbed the muzzle blindly against the dog's body. He pulled and pulled the trigger until the roars died away and only empty clicks sounded. Umber shuddered in the ashes before him, his body nearly shot in two. Thick scarlet stained the gray.

Evelyn and Hallmyer looked down sadly at the broken animal. Evelyn was crying, and Hallmyer reached nervous fingers through his hair in the same old gesture.

"This is the finish, Steven," he said. "You've killed part of yourself. Oh—you'll go on living, but not all of you. You'd best bury that body, Steven. It's the corpse of your soul."

"I can't," Krane said. "The wind will blow the cinders away."

"Then burn it," Hallmyer ordered with dream-logic.

It seemed that they helped him thrust the dead dog into his knapsack. They helped him take off his clothes and packed them underneath. They cupped their hands around the matches until the cloth caught fire, and blew on the weak flame until it sputtered and burned limply. Krane crouched by the fire and nursed it. Then he turned and once again began crawling down the ocean bed. He was naked now. There was nothing left of what-had-been but his flickering little life.

He was too heavy with sorrow to notice the furious rain that slammed and buffeted him, or the searing pains that were searing through his blackened leg and up his hip. He crawled. Elbows, knee, elbows, knee— Woodenly, mechanically, apathetic to everything . . . to the latticed skies, the dreary ashen plains and even the dull glint of water that lay far ahead.

He knew it was the sea—what was left of the old, or a new one in the making. But it would be an empty, lifeless sea that some day would lap against a dry, lifeless shore. This would be a planet of stone and dust, of metal and snow and ice and water, but that would be all. No more life. He, alone, was useless. He was Adam, but there was no Eve.

Evelyn waved gaily to him from the shore. She was standing alongside the white cottage with the wind snapping her dress to show the slender lines of her figure. And when he came a little closer, she ran out to him and helped him. She said nothing—only placed her hands under his shoulders and helped him lift the weight of his heavy pain-ridden body. And so at last he reached the sea.

It was real. He understood that. For even after Evelyn and the cottage had vanished, he felt the cool waters bathe his face.

Here's the sea, Krane thought, and here am I. Adam and no Eve. It's hopeless.

He rolled a little farther into the waters. They laved his torn body. He lay with face to the sky, peering at the high menacing heavens, and the bitterness within him welled up.

"It's not right!" he cried. "It's not right that all this should pass away. Life is too beautiful to perish at the mad act of one mad creature—"

Quietly the waters laved him. Quietly . . . Calmly . . .

The sea rocked him gently, and even the death that was reaching up toward his heart was no more than a gloved hand. Suddenly the skies split apart—for the first time in all those months—and Krane stared up at the stars.

Then he knew. This was not the end of life. There could never be an end to life. Within his body, within the rotting tissues rocking gently in the sea was the source of ten million-million lives. Cells—tissues—bacteria—amoeba— Countless infinities of life that would take new root in the waters and live long after he was gone.

They would live on his rotting remains. They would feed on each other. They would adapt themselves to the new environment and feed on the minerals and sediments washed into this new sea. They would grow, burgeon, evolve. Life would reach out to the lands once more. It would begin again the same old repeated cycle that had begun perhaps with the rotting corpse of some last survivor of interstellar travel. It would happen over and over in the future ages.

And then he knew what had brought him back to the sea. There need be no Adam—no Eve. Only the sea, the great mother of life was needed. The sea had called him back to her depths that presently life might emerge once more, and he was content.

Quietly the waters comforted him. Quietly . . . Calmly . . . The mother of life rocked the last-born of the old cycle who would become the first-born of the new. And with glazing eyes Steven Krane smiled up at the stars, stars that were sprinkled evenly across the sky. Stars that had not yet formed into the familiar constellations, and would not for another hundred million centuries.

Star Light, Star Bright

THE MAN IN THE CAR WAS THIRTY-EIGHT YEARS OLD. He was tall, slender, and not strong. His cropped hair was prematurely gray. He was afflicted with an education and a sense of humor. He was inspired by a purpose. He was armed with a phone book. He was doomed.

He drove up Post Avenue, stopped at No. 17 and parked. He consulted the phone book, then got out of the car and entered the house. He examined the mail boxes and then ran up the stairs to apartment 2-F. He rang the bell. While he waited for an answer he got out a small black notebook and a superior silver pencil that wrote in four colors.

The door opened. To a nondescript middle-aged lady, the man said: "Good evening. Mrs. Buchanan?"

The lady nodded.

"My name is Foster. I'm from the Science Institute. We're trying to check some flying saucer reports. I won't take a minute." Mr. Foster insinuated himself into the apartment. He had been in so many that he knew the layout automatically. He marched briskly down the hall to the front parlor, turned, smiled at Mrs. Buchanan, opened the notebook to a blank page and poised the pencil.

"Have you ever seen a flying saucer, Mrs. Buchanan?"

"No. And it's a lot of bunk. I—"

"Have your children ever seen them? You do have children?"

"Yeah, but they—"

"How many?"

"Two. Them flying saucers never—"

"Are either of school age?"

"What?"

"School," Mr. Foster repeated impatiently. "Do they go to school?"

"The boy's twenty-eight," Mrs. Buchanan said. "The girl's twenty-four. They finished school a long—"

"I see. Either of them married?"

"No. About them flying saucers, you scientist doctors ought to—"

38

"We are," Mr. Foster interrupted. He made a tick-tack-toe in the notebook, then closed it and slid it into an inside pocket with the pencil. "Thank you very much, Mrs. Buchanan," he said, turned, and marched out.

Downstairs, Mr. Foster got into the car, opened the telephone directory, turned to a page and ran his pencil through a name. He examined the name underneath, memorized the address and started the car. He drove to Fort George Avenue and stopped the car in front of No. 800. He entered the house and took the self-service elevator to the fourth floor. He rang the bell of apartment 4-G. While he waited for an answer he got out the small black notebook and the superior pencil.

The door opened. To a truculent man, Mr. Foster said, "Good-evening. Mr. Buchanan?"

"What about it?" the truculent man said.

Mr. Foster said, "My name is Davis. I'm from the Association of National Broadcasters. "We're preparing a list of names for prize competitors. May I come in? Won't take a minute."

Mr. Foster/Davis insinuated himself and presently consulted with Mr. Buchanan and his redheaded wife in the living room of their apartment.

"Have you ever won a prize in radio or television?"

"No," Mr. Buchanan said angrily. "We never got a chance. Everybody else does but not us."

"All that free money and iceboxes," Mrs. Buchanan said. "Trips to Paris and planes and—"

"That's why we're making up this list," Mr. Foster/Davis broke in. "Have any of your relatives won prizes?"

"No. It's all a fix. Put-up jobs. They—"

"Any of your children?"

"Ain't got any children."

"I see. Thank you very much." Mr. Foster/Davis played out the tick-tack-toe game in his notebook, closed it and put it away. He released himself from the indignation of the Buchanans, went down to his car crossed out another name in the phone book, memorized the address of the name underneath and started the car.

He drove to No. 1215 East Sixty-eighth Street and parked in front of a private brownstone house. He rang the doorbell and was confronted by a maid in uniform.

"Good evening," he said. "Is Mr. Buchanan in?"

"Who's calling?"

"My name is Hook," Mr. Foster/Davis said. "I'm conducting an investigation for the Better Business Bureau."

The maid disappeared, reappeared and conducted Mr. Foster/Davis/Hook to a small library where a resolute gentleman in dinner clothes stood holding a Limoges demitasse cup and saucer. There were expensive books on the shelves. There was an expensive fire in the grate.

"Mr. Hook?"

"Yes, sir," the doomed man replied. He did not take out the notebook. "I won't be a minute, Mr. Buchanan. Just a few questions."

"I have great faith in the Better Business Bureau," Mr. Buchanan pronounced. "Our bulwark against the inroads of—"

"Thank you, sir," Mr. Foster/Davis/Hook interrupted. "Have you ever been criminally defrauded by a business man?"

"The attempt has been made. I have never succumbed."

"And your children? You do have children?"

"My son is hardly old enough to qualify as a victim."

"How old is he, Mr. Buchanan?"

"Ten."

"Perhaps he has been tricked at school? There are crooks who specialize in victimizing children."

"Not at my son's school. He is well protected."

"What school is that, sir?"

"Germanson."

"One of the best. Did he ever attend a city public school?"

"Never."

The doomed man took out the notebook and the superior pencil. This time he made a serious entry.

"Any other children, Mr. Buchanan?"

"A daughter, seventeen."

Mr. Foster/Davis/Hook considered, started to write, changed his mind and closed the notebook. He thanked his host politely and escaped from the house before Mr. Buchanan could ask for his credentials. He was ushered out by the maid, ran down the stoop to his car, opened the door, entered and was felled by a tremendous blow on the side of his head.

When the doomed man awoke, he thought he was in bed suffering from a hangover. He started to crawl to the bathroom when he realized he was dumped in a chair like a suit for the cleaners. He opened his eyes. He was in what appeared to be an underwater grotto. He blinked frantically. The water receded.

He was in a small legal office. A stout man who looked like an unfrocked Santa Claus stood before him. To one side, seated on a desk and swinging his legs carelessly, was a thin young man with a lantern jaw and eyes closely set on either side of his nose.

"Can you hear me?" the stout man asked.

The doomed man grunted.

"Can we talk?"

Another grunt.

"Joe," the stout man said pleasantly, "a towel."

The thin young man slipped off the desk, went to a corner basin and soaked a white hand towel. He shook it once, sauntered back to the chair where, with the suddenness and savagery of a tiger, he lashed it across the sick man's face.

"For God's sake!" Mr. Foster/Davis/Hook cried.

"That's better," the stout man said. "My name's Herod. Walter Herod, attorney-at-law." He stepped to the desk where the contents of the doomed man's pockets were spread, picked up a wallet and displayed it. "Your name is Warbeck. Marion Perkin Warbeck. Right?"

The doomed man gazed at his wallet, then at Walter Herod, attorney-at-law, and finally admitted the truth. "Yes," he said. "My name is Warbeck. But I never admit the Marion to strangers."

He was again lashed by the wet towel and fell back in the chair, stung and bewildered.

"That will do, Joe," Herod said. "Not again, please, until I tell you." To Warbeck he said, "Why this interest in the Buchanans?" He waited for an answer, then continued pleasantly, "Joe's been tailing you. You've averaged five Buchanans a night. Thirty so far. What's your angle?"

"What the hell is this? Russia?" Warbeck demanded indignantly. "You've got no right to kidnap me and grill me like the MVD. If you think you can—"

"Joe," Herod interrupted pleasantly. "Again, please."

Again the towel lashed Warbeck. Tormented, furious and helpless, he burst into tears.

Herod fingered the wallet casually. "Your papers say you're a teacher by profession, principal of a public school. I thought teachers were supposed to be legit. How did you get mixed up in the inheritance racket?"

"The what racket?" Warbeck asked faintly.

"The inheritance racket," Herod repeated patiently. "The Heirs of Buchanan caper. What kind of parlay are you using? Personal approach?"

"I don't know what you're talking about," Warbeck answered. He sat bolt upright and pointed to the thin youth. "And don't start that towel business again."

"I'll start what I please and when I please," Herod said ferociously. "And I'll finish you when I goddamned well please. You're stepping on my toes and I don't buy it. I've got seventy-five-thousand a year I'm taking out of this and I'm not going to let you chisel."

There was a long pause, significant for everybody in the room except the doomed man. Finally he spoke. "I'm an educated man," he said slowly. "Mention Galileo, say, or the lesser Cavalier poets, and I'm right up there with you. But there are gaps in my education and this is one of them. I can't meet the situation. Too many unknowns."

"I told you my name," Herod answered. He pointed to the thin young man. "That's Joe Davenport."

Warbeck shook his head. "Unknown in the mathematical sense. X quantities. Solving equations. My education speaking."

Joe looked startled. "Jesus!" he said without moving his lips. "Maybe he *is* legit."

Herod examined Warbeck curiously. "I'm going to spell it out for you," he said. "The inheritance racket is a long-term con. It operates something like so: There's a story that James Buchanan—"

"Fifteenth President of the U.S.?"

"In person. There's a story he died intestate leaving an estate for heirs unknown. That was in 1868. Today at compound interest that estate is worth millions. Understand?"

Warbeck nodded. "I'm educated," he murmured.

"Anybody named Buchanan is a sucker for this setup. It's a switch on the Spanish Prisoner routine. I send them a letter. Tell 'em there's a chance they may be one of the heirs. Do they want me to investigate and protect their cut in the estate? It only costs a small yearly retainer. Most of them buy it. From all over the country. And now you—"

"Wait a minute," Warbeck exclaimed. "I can draw a conclusion. You found out I was checking the Buchanan families. You think I'm trying to operate the same racket. Cut in . . . cut in? Yes? Cut in on you?"

"Well," Herod asked angrily, "aren't you?"

"Oh God!" Warbeck cried. "That this should happen to me. Me! Thank You, God. Thank You. I'll always be grateful." In his happy fervor he turned to Joe. "Give me the towel Joe," he said. "Just throw it. I've got to wipe my face." He caught the flung towel and mopped himself joyously.

"Well," Herod repeated. "Aren't you?"

"No," Warbeck answered, "I'm not cutting in on you. But I'm grateful for the mistake. Don't think I'm not. You can't imagine how flattering it is for a schoolteacher to be taken for a thief."

He got out of the chair and went to the desk to reclaim his wallet and other possessions.

"Just a minute," Herod snapped.

The thin young man reached out and grasped Warbeck's wrist with an iron clasp.

"Oh stop it," the doomed man said impatiently. "This is a silly mistake."

"I'll tell you whether it's a mistake and I'll tell you if it's silly," Herod replied. "Just now you'll do as you're told."

"Will I?" Warbeck wrenched his wrist free and slashed Joe across the eyes with the towel. He darted around behind the desk, snatched up a paper weight and hurled it through the window with a shattering crash.

"Joe!" Herod yelled.

Warbeck knocked the phone off its stand and dialed Operator. He picked up his cigarette lighter, flicked it and dropped it into the wastepaper basket. The voice of the operator buzzed in the phone. Warbeck shouted, "I want a policeman!" Then he kicked the flaming basket into the center of the office.

"Joe!" Herod yelled and stamped on the blazing paper.

Warbeck grinned. He picked up the phone. Squawking noises were coming out of it. He put one hand over the mouthpiece. "Shall we negotiate?" he inquired.

"You son of a bitch," Joe growled. He took his hands from his eyes and slid toward Warbeck.

"No!" Herod called. "This crazy fool's hollered copper. He's legit, Joe." To Warbeck he said in pleading tones, "Fix it. Square it. We'll make it up to you. Anything you say. Just square the call."

The doomed man lifted the phone to his mouth. He said, "My name is M. P. Warbeck. I was consulting my attorney at this number and some idiot with a misplaced sense of humor made this call. Please phone back and check."

He hung up, finished pocketing his private property and winked at Herod. The phone rang. Warbeck picked it up, reassured the police and hung up. He came around from behind the desk and handed his car keys to Joe.

"Go down to my car," he said. "You know where you parked it. Open the glove compartment and bring up a brown manila envelope you'll find."

"Go to hell," Joe spat. His eyes were still tearing.

"Do as I say," Warbeck said firmly.

"Just a minute, Warbeck," Herod said. "What's this? A new angle? I said we'd make it up to you, but—"

"I'm going to explain why I'm interested in the Buchanans," Warbeck replied. "And I'm going into partnership with you. You've got what I need to locate one particular Buchanan . . . you and Joe. My Buchanan's ten years old. He's worth a hundred times your make-believe fortune."

Herod stared at him.

Warbeck placed the keys in Joe's hand. "Go down and get that envelope, Joe," he said. "And while you're at it you'd better square that broken window rap. Rap? Rap."

The doomed man placed the manila envelope neatly on his lap. "A school principal," he explained, "has to supervise school classes. He reviews work, estimates progress, irons out student problems and so on. This must be done at random. By samplings, I mean. I have nine-hundred pupils in my school. I can't supervise them individually."

Herod nodded. Joe looked blank.

"Looking through some fifth grade work last month," Warbeck continued, "I came across this astonishing document." He opened the envelope and took out a few sheets of ruled composition paper covered with blots and scrawled writing. "It was written by a Stuart Buchanan of the fifth grade. His age must be ten or thereabouts. The composition is entitled: *My Vacation*. Read it and you'll understand why Stuart Buchanan must be found."

He tossed the sheets to Herod who picked them up, took out a pair of horn-rim spectacles and balanced them

on his fat nose. Joe came around to the back of his
chair and peered over his shoulder.

My Vacatoin
by
Stuart Buchanan

*This sumer I vissited my frends. I have 4 frends
and they are verry nice. First there is Tommy who
lives in the contry and he is an astronnimer. Tommy
bilt his own tellescop out of glass 6 inches acros wich
he grond himself. He loks at the stars every nihgt and he
let me lok even wen it was raining cats & dogs . . .*

"What the hell?" Herod looked up, annoyed.
"Read on. Read on," Warbeck said.

*cats & dogs. We cold see the stars becaze Tommy
made a thing for over the end of the tellescop wich
shoots up like a serchlite and makes a hole in the skie
to see rite thru the rain and everythinng to the stars.*

"Finished the astronomer yet?" Warbeck inquired.
"I don't dig it."
"Tommy got bored waiting for clear nights. He invented something that cuts through clouds and atmosphere . . . a funnel of vacuum so he can use his tele-
scope all weather. What it amounts to is a disintegration
beam."
"The hell you say."
"The hell I don't. Read on. Read on."

*Then I went to AnnMary and staied one hole week.
It was fun. Becaze AnnMary has a spinak chainger
for spinak and beats and strinbeens—*

"What the hell is a 'spinak chainger'?"
"Spinach. Spinach changer. Spelling isn't one of Stuart's
specialties. 'Beasts' are beets. 'Strinbeens' are string
beans."

*beats and strinbeens. Wen her mother made us eet
them AnnMary presed the buton and they staid the
same outside onnly inside they became cake. Chery
and strowbery. I asted AnnMary how & she sed it was
by Enhv.*

"This, I don't get."

"Simple. Anne-Marie doesn't like vegetables. So she's just as smart as Tommy, the astronomer. She invented a matter-transmuter. She transmutes spinak into cake. Chery or strowbery. Cake she eats with pleasure. So does Stuart."

"You're crazy."

"Not me. The kids. They're geniuses. Geniuses? What am I saying? They make a genius look imbecile. There's no label for these children."

"I don't believe it. This Stuart Buchanan's got a tall imagination. That's all."

"You think so? Then what about Enhv? That's how Anne-Marie transmutes matter. It took time but I figured Enhv out. It's Planck's quantum equation $E-nhv$. But read on. Read on. The best is yet to come. Wait till you get to lazy Ethel."

My frend Gorge bilds modell airplanes very good and small. Gorg's hands are clumzy but he makes small men out of moddelling clay and he tels them and they bild for him.

"What's this?"

"George, the plane-maker?"

"Yes."

"Simple. He makes miniature androids . . . robots . . . and they build the planes for him. Clever boy, George, but read about his sister, lazy Ethel."

His sister Ethel is the lazyist girl I ever saw. She is big & fat and she hates to walk. So wen her mothar sends her too the store Ethel thinks to the store and thinks home with all the pakejes and has to hang arownd Gorg's room hiding untill it wil look like she walked both ways. Gorge and I make fun of her becaze she is fat and lazy but she gets into the movees for free and saw Hoppalong Casidy sixteen times.

The End

Herod stared at Warbeck.

"Great little girl, Ethel," Warbeck said. "She's too lazy to walk so she teleports. Then she has a devil of a time covering up. She has to hide with her pakejes while George and Stuart make fun of her."

"Teleports?"

"That's right. She moves from place to place by thinking her way there."

"There ain't no such thing!" Joe said indignantly.

"There wasn't until lazy Ethel came along."

"I don't believe this," Herod said. "I don't believe any of it."

"You think it's just Stuart's imagination?"

"What else?"

"What about Planck's equation? $E=nh\nu$?"

"The kid invented that too. Coincidence."

"Does that sound likely?"

"Then he read it somewhere."

"A ten-year-old boy? Nonsense."

"I tell you, I don't believe it," Herod shouted. "Let me talk to the kid for five minutes and I'll prove it."

"That's exactly what I want to do . . . only the boy's disappeared."

"How do you mean?"

"Lock, stock and barrel. That's why I've been checking every Buchanan family in the city. The day I read this composition and sent down to the fifth grade for Stuart Buchanan to have a talk, he disappeared. He hasn't been seen since."

"What about his family?"

"The family disappeared too." Warbeck leaned forward intensely. "Get this. Every record of the boy and the family disappeared. Everything. A few people remember them vaguely, but that's all. They're gone."

"Jesus!" Joe said. "They scrammed, huh?"

"The very word. Scrammed. Thank you, Joe." Warbeck cocked an eye at Herod. "What a situation. Here's a child who makes friends with child geniuses. And the emphasis is on the child. They're making fantastic discoveries for childish purposes. Ethel teleports because she's too lazy to run errands. George makes robots to build model planes. Anne-Marie transmutes elements because she hates spinach. God knows what Stuart's other friends are doing. Maybe there's a Matthew who's invented a time machine so he can catch up on his homework."

Herod waved his hands feebly. "Why geniuses all of a sudden? What's happened?"

"I don't know. Atomic fall-out? Fluorides in drinking water? Antibiotics? Vitamins? We're doing so much juggling with body chemistry these days that who knows what's happening? I want to find out but I can't. Stuart Buchanan blabbed like a child. When I started investigating he got scared and disappeared."

"Is he a genius too?"

"Very likely. Kids generally hang out with kids who share the same interests and talents."

"What kind of a genius? What's his talent?"

"I don't know. All I know is he disappeared. He covered up his tracks, destroyed every paper that could possibly help me locate him and vanished into thin air."

"How did he get into your files?"

"I don't know."

"Maybe he's a crook type," Joe said. "Expert at breaking and entering and such."

Herod smiled wanly. "A racketeer genius? A mastermind? The kid Moriarty?"

"He could be a thief-genius," the doomed man said, "but don't let running away convince you. All children do that when they get caught in a crisis. Either they wish it had never happened or they wish they were a million miles away. Stuart Buchanan may be a million miles away but we've got to find him."

"Just to find out is he smart?" Joe asked.

"No, to find his friends. Do I have to diagram it? What would the army pay for a disintegration beam? What would an element-transmuter be worth? If we could manufacture living robots how rich would we get? If we could teleport how powerful would we be?"

There was a burning silence, then Herod got to his feet. "Mr. Warbeck," he said, "you make me and Joe look like pikers. Thank you for letting us cut in on you. We'll pay off. We'll find that kid."

It is not possible for anyone to vanish without a trace . . . even a probable criminal genius. It is sometimes difficult to locate that trace . . . even for an expert experienced in hurried disappearances. But there is a professional technique unknown to amateurs.

"You've been blundering," Herod explained kindly to the doomed man. "Chasing one Buchanan after the other. There are angles. You don't run after a missing party. You look around on his back-trail for something he dropped."

"A genius wouldn't drop anything."

"Let's grant the kid's a genius. Type unspecified. Let's grant him everything. But a kid is a kid. He must have overlooked something. We'll find it."

In three days Warbeck was introduced to the most

astonishing angles of search. They consulted the Washington Heights post office about a Buchanan family formerly living in that neighborhood, now moved. Was there any change-of-address-card filed? None.

They visited the election board. All voters are registered by wards. If a voter moves from one election district to another, provision is usually made that a record of the transfer be kept. Was there any such record on Buchanan? None.

They called on the Washington Heights office of the gas and electric company. All subscribers for gas and electricity must transfer their accounts if they move. If they move out of town, they generally request the return of their deposit. Was there any record of a party named Buchanan? None.

It is a state law that all drivers must notify the license bureau of change of address or be subject to penalties involving fines, prison or worse. Was there any such notification by a party named Buchanan at the Motor Vehicle Bureau? There was not.

They questioned the R-J Realty Corp., owners and operators of a multiple dwelling in Washington Heights in which a party named Buchanan had leased a four-room apartment. The R-J lease, like most other leases, required the names and addresses of two character references for the tenant. Could the character references for Buchanan be produced? They could not. There was no such lease in the files.

"Maybe Joe was right," Warbeck complained in Herod's office. "Maybe the boy is a thief-genius. How did he think of everything? How did he get at every paper and destroy it? Did he break and enter? Bribe? Burgle? Threaten? How did he do it?"

"We'll ask him when we get to him," Herod said grimly. "All right. The kid's licked us straight down the line. He hasn't forgotten a trick. But I've got one angle I've been saving. Let's go up and see the janitor of their building."

"I questioned him months ago," Warbeck objected. "He remembers the family in a vague way and that's all. He doesn't know where they went."

"He knows something else, something the kid wouldn't think of covering. Let's go get it."

They drove up to Washington Heights and descended upon Mr. Jacob Ruysdale at dinner in the basement apartment of the building. Mr. Ruysdale disliked being separated from his liver and onions but was persuaded by five dollars.

"About that Buchanan family," Herod began.

"I told him everything before," Ruysdale broke in, pointing to Warbeck.

"All right. He forgot to ask one question. Can I ask it now?" Ruysdale re-examined the five-dollar bill and nodded.

"When anybody moves in or out of a building, the superintendent usually takes down the name of the movers in case they damage the building. I'm a lawyer. I know this. It's to protect the building in case suit has to be brought. Right?"

Ruysdale's face lit up. "By Godfrey!" he said. "That's right, I forgot all about it. He never asked me."

"He didn't know. You've got the name of the company that moved the Buchanans out. Right?"

Ruysdale ran across the room to a cluttered bookshelf. He withdrew a tattered journal and flipped it open. He wet his fingers and turned pages.

"Here it is," he said. "The Avon Moving Company. Truck No. G-4."

The Avon Moving Company had no record of the removal of a Buchanan family from an apartment in Washington Heights. "The kid was pretty careful at that," Herod murmured. But it did have a record of the men working truck G-4 on that day. The men were interviewed when they checked in at closing time. Their memories were refreshed with whiskey and cash. They recalled the Washington Heights job vaguely. It was a full day's work because they had to drive the hell and gone to Brooklyn. "Oh God! Brooklyn!" Warbeck muttered. What address in Brooklyn? Something on Maple Park Row. Number? The number could not be recalled.

"Joe, buy a map."

They examined the street map of Brooklyn and located Maple Park Row. It was indeed the hell and gone out of civilization and was twelve blocks long. "That's *Brooklyn* blocks," Joe grunted. "Twice as long as anywhere. I know."

Herod shrugged. "We're close," he said. "The rest will have to be leg work. Four blocks apiece. Cover every house, every apartment. List every kid around ten. Then Warbeck can check them, if they're under an alias."

"There's a million kids a square inch in Brooklyn." Joe protested.

"There's a million dollars a day in it for us if we find him. Now let's go."

Maple Park Row was a long crooked street lined with five-story apartment houses. Its sidewalks were lined with baby carriages and old ladies on camp chairs. Its curbs were lined with parked cars. Its gutter was lined with crude whitewash stickball courts shaped like elongated diamonds. Every manhole cover was a home plate.

"It's just like the Bronx," Joe said nostalgically. "I ain't been home to the Bronx in ten years."

He wandered sadly down the street toward his sector, automatically threading his way through stickball games with the unconscious skill of the city-born. Warbeck remembered that departure sympathetically because Joe Davenport never returned.

The first day, he and Herod imagined Joe had found a hot lead. This encouraged them. The second day they realized no heat could keep Joe on the fire for forty-eight hours. This depressed them. On the third day they had to face the truth.

"He's dead," Herod said flatly. "The kid got him."

"How?"

"He killed him."

"A ten-year-old boy? A child?"

"You want to know what kind of genius Stuart Buchanan has, don't you? I'm telling you."

"I don't believe it."

"Then explain Joe."

"He quit."

"Not on a million dollars."

"But where's the body?"

"Ask the kid. He's the genius. He's probably figured out tricks that would baffle Dick Tracy."

"How did he kill him?"

"Ask the kid. He's the genius."

"Herod, I'm scared."

"So am I. Do you want to quit now?"

"I don't see how we can. If the boy's dangerous we've got to find him."

"Civic virtue, heh?"

"Call it that."

"Well, I'm still thinking about the money."

They returned to Maple Park Row and Joe Davenport's four-block sector. They were cautious, almost furtive. They separated and began working from each end toward the middle; in one house, up the stairs, apartment by apartment, to the top, then down again to investigate the next building. It was slow, tedious work. Occasionally they glimpsed each other far down the street, crossing from one dismal building to another. And that was the last glimpse Warbeck ever had of Walter Herod.

He sat in his car and waited. He sat in his car and trembled. "I'll go to the police," he muttered, knowing perfectly well he could not. "The boy has a weapon. Something he invented. Something silly like the others. A special light so he can play marbles at night, only it murders men. A machine to play checkers, only it hypnotizes men. He's invented a robot mob of gangsters so he can play cops-and-robbers and they took care of Joe and Herod. He's a child genius. Dangerous. Deadly. What am I going to do."

The doomed man got out of the car and stumbled down the street toward Herod's half of the sector. "What's going to happen when Stuart Buchanan grows up?" he wondered. "What's going to happen when all the rest of them grow up? Tommy and George and Anne-Marie and lazy Ethel? Why don't I start running away now? What am I doing here?"

It was dusk on Maple Park Row. The old ladies had withdrawn, folding their camp chairs like Arabs. The parked cars remained. The stickball games were over, but small games were starting under the glowing lamp posts . . . games with bottle caps and cards and battered pennies. Overhead, the purple city haze was deepening, and through it the sharp sparkle of Venus following the sun below the horizon could be seen.

"He must know his power," Warbeck muttered angrily. "He must know how dangerous he is. That's why he's running away. Guilt. That's why he destroys us, one by one, smiling to himself, a crafty child, a vicious, killing genius. . . ."

Warbeck stopped in the middle of Maple Park Row.

"Buchanan!" he shouted. "Stuart Buchanan!"

The kids near him stopped their games and gaped.

"Stuart Buchanan!" Warbeck's voice cracked hysterically. "Can you hear me?"

His wild voice carried farther down the street. More

games stopped. Ringaleevio, Chinese tag, Red-Light and Boxball.

"Buchanan!" Warbeck screamed. "Stuart Buchanan! Come out come out, wherever you are!"

The world hung motionless.

In the alley between 217 and 219 Maple Park Row, playing hide-and-seek behind piled ash barrels, Stuart Buchanan heard his name and crouched lower. He was aged ten, dressed in sweater, jeans and sneakers. He was intent and determined that he was not going to be caught out "it" again. He was going to hide until he could make a dash for home-free in safety. As he settled comfortably among the ash cans, his eye caught the glimmer of Venus low in the western sky.

"Star light, star bright," he whispered in all innocence, "first star I see tonight. Wish I may, wish I might, grant me the wish I wish tonight." He paused and considered. Then he wished. "God bless Mom and Pop and me and all my friends and make me a good boy and please let me be always happy and I wish that anybody who tries to bother me would go away . . . a long way away . . . and leave me alone forever."

In the middle of Maple Park Row, Marion Perkin Warbeck stepped forward and drew breath for another hysterical yell. And then he was elsewhere, going away on a road that was a long way away. It was a straight white road cleaving infinitely through blackness, stretching onward and onward into forever; a dreary, lonely, endless road leading away and away and away.

Down that road Warbeck plodded, an astonished automaton, unable to speak, unable to stop, unable to think in the timeless infinity. Onward and onward he walked into a long way away, unable to turn back. Ahead of him he saw the minute specks of figures trapped on that one-way road to forever. There was a dot that had to be Herod. Ahead of Herod was a mote that was Joe Davenport. And ahead of Joe he could make out a long dwindling chain of mites. He turned once with a convulsive effort. Behind him, dim and distant, a figure was plodding, and behind that another abruptly materialized, and another . . . and another. . . .

While Stuart Buchanan crouched behind the ash barrels and watched alertly for the "it." He was unaware that he had disposed of Warbeck. He was unaware that he had disposed of Herod, Joe Davenport and scores of others.

He was unaware that he had induced his parents to flee Washington Heights, that he had destroyed papers and documents, memories and peoples in his simple desire to be left alone. He was unaware that he was a genius.

His genius was for wishing.

✳

The Roller Coaster

I KNIFED HER A LITTLE. WHEN YOU CUT ACROSS THE ribs it hurts like sin but it isn't dangerous. The knife slash showed white, then red. She backed away from me in astonishment, more startled at the knife than the cut. You don't feel those cuts at first for quite a few minutes. That's the trouble with a knife. It numbs and the pain comes slow.

"Listen, lover," I said. (I'd forgotten her name.) "This is what I've got for you. Look at it." I waggled the knife. "Feel it." I slapped her across the face with the blade. She stumbled back against the couch, sat down and began to shake. This was what I was waiting for.

"Go ahead, you bitch. Answer me."

"Please, David," she muttered.

Dull. Not so good.

"I'm on my way out," I said. "You lousy hooker. You're like all the rest of these cheap dames."

"Please, David," she repeated in a low voice.

No action here. Give her one more try.

"Figuring you for two dollars a night, I'm into you for twenty." I took money from my pocket, stripped off the twenty in singles and handed it to her. She wouldn't touch it. She sat on the edge of the couch, blue-naked, streaming blood, not looking at me. Just dull. And mind you a girl that made love with her teeth. She used to scratch me with her nails like a cat. And now . . .

"Please, David," she said.

I tore up the money and threw it in her lap.

"Please, David," she said.

No tears. No screams. No action. She was impossible. I walked out.

The whole trouble with these neurotics is that you can't depend on them. You case them. You work them. You build to the climax. You trigger them off, but as often as not they dummy up like that girl. You just can't figure them.

I looked at my watch. The hand was on twelve. I decided to go up to Gandry's apartment. Freyda was working Gandry and would most likely be there setting him up for the climax. I needed advice from Freyda and I didn't have much time left.

I walked north on Sixth Avenue—no, The Avenue of the Americas; turned west on Fifty-fifth and went to the house across the street from Mecca Temple—no, The New York City Center. I took the elevator up to the PH floor and was just going to ring Gandry's bell when I smelled gas. I knelt down and sniffed at the edge of Gandry's door. It was coming from his apartment.

I knew better than to ring the bell. I got out my keys, touched them to the elevator call-button to dissipate any electrostatic charge on them, and got to work on Gandry's door. I barbered the lock in two or three minutes, opened the door and went in with my handkerchief over my nose. The place was pitch dark. I went straight to the kitchen and stumbled over a body lying on the floor with its head in the oven. I turned off the gas and opened the window. I ran into the living room and opened windows. I stuck my head out for a breath, then came back and finished airing the apartment.

I checked the body. It was Gandry all right. He was still alive. His big face was swollen and purple and his breathing sounded a little Cheynes-Stokesish to me. I went to the phone and dialed Freyda.

"Hello?"

"Freyda?"

"Yes?"

"Where are you? Why aren't you up here with Gandry?"

"Is that you, David?"

"Yes. I just broke in and found Gandry half dead. He's trying suicide."

"Oh, David!"

"Gas. He's reached the climax all by his lonely lone self. You been building him?"

"Of course, but I never thought he'd—"

"He'd try to sneak out on the pay-off like this? I've told you a hundred times, Freyda. You can't depend on potential suicides like Gandry. I showed you those trial-cut scars on his wrist. His kind never give you any action. They—"

"Don't lecture me, David."

"Never mind. My girl was a bust, too. I thought she was the hot acid type. She turned out to be mush. I want to try that Bacon woman you mentioned. Would you rec-ommend her?"

"Definitely."

"How can I find her?"

"Through her husband, Eddie Bacon."

"How can I find him?"

"Try Shawn's or Dugal's or Breen's or The Greek's. But he's a talker, David, a time-waster; and you haven't much time left."

"Doesn't matter if his wife's worth it."

"She's worth it, David. I told you about the gun."

"Right. Now what about Gandry?"

"Oh, to hell with Gandry," she snapped, and hung up.

That was all right with me. It was about time Freyda got sense enough to lay off the psychotics. I hung up, closed all the windows, went back to the kitchen and turned on the gas. Gandry hadn't moved. I put out all the lights, went down the hall and let myself out.

I went looking for Eddie Bacon. I tried for him at Breen's, at Shawn's, at Dugal's. I got the break at The Greek's on East Fifty-second Street.

I asked the bartender: "Is Eddie Bacon here?"

"In the back."

I looked past the juke box. The back was crowded. "Which one is Eddie Bacon?"

He pointed to a small man alone at a table in the cor-ner. I went back and sat down. "Hi, Eddie."

Bacon glanced up at me. He had a seamed, pouchy face, fair silky hair, bleak blue eyes. He wore a brown suit and a blue and white polka dot tie. He caught me looking at the tie and said: "That's the tie I wear be-tween wars. What are you drinking?"

"Scotch. Water. No ice."

"How English can you get?" He yelled: "Chris!"

I got my drink. "Where's Liz?"

"Who?"

"Your wife."

"I married eighteen feet of wives," he mumbled. "End to end. Six feet each."

"Three fathoms of show girls," I said.

"Which were you referring to?"

"The third. The most recent. I hear she left you."

"They all left me."

"Where's Liz?"

"It happened like this," Bacon said in a sullen voice. "I can't figure it. Nobody can figure it. I took the kids to Coney Island . . ."

"Never mind the kids. Where's Liz?"

"I'm getting there," Bacon said irritably. "Coney Island's the damnedest place. Everybody ought to try that trap once. It's primitive stuff. Basic entertainment. They scare the hell out of your glands and you love it. Appeals to the ancient history in us. The Cro-Magnons and all that."

"The Cro-Magnons died out," I said. "You mean the Neanderthals."

"I mean prehistoric memories," Bacon went on. "They strap you into that roller coaster, they shove you off and you drop into a race with a dinosaur. He's chasing you and you're trying to keep it from ending in a dead heat. Basic. It appeals to the Stone Age flesh in us. That's why kids dig it. Every kid's a vestigial remnant from the Stone Age."

"Grown-ups too. What about Liz?"

"Chris!" Bacon yelled. Another round of drinks came. "Yeah . . . Liz," he said. "The girl made me forget there ever was a Liz. I met her staggering off the roller coaster. She was waiting. Waiting to pounce. The Black Widow Spider."

"Liz?"

"No. The little whore that wasn't there."

"Who?"

"Haven't you heard about Bacon's Missing Mistress? The Invisible Lay? Bacon's Thinking Affair?"

"No."

"Hell, where've you been? How Bacon rented an apartment for a dame that didn't exist. They're still laughing it up. All except Liz. It's all over the business."

"I'm not in your business."

"No?" He took a long drink, put his glass down and glowered at the table like a kid trying to crack an alge-

bra problem. "Her name was Freyda. F-R-E-Y-D-A.
Like Freya, Goddess of Spring. Eternal youth. She was
like a Botticelli virgin outside. She was a tiger inside."

"Freyda what?"

"I don't know. I never found out. Maybe she didn't
have any last name because she was imaginary like they
keep telling me." He took a deep breath. "I do a crime
show on TV. I know every crook routine there is. That's
my business—the thief business. But she pulled a new
one. She picked me up by pretending she'd met the kids
somewhere. Who can tell if a kid really knows someone
or not? They're only half human anyway. I swallowed
her routine. By the time I realized she was lying, I'd
met her and I was dead. She had me on the hook."

"How do you mean?"

"A wife is a wife," Bacon said. "Three wives are
just more of the same. But this was going to bed with a
tiger." He smiled sourly. "Only it's all my imagination,
they keep telling me. It's all inside my head. I never really
killed her because she never really lived."

"You killed her? Freyda?"

"It was a war from the start," he said, "and it ended up
with a killing. It wasn't love with her, it was war."

"This is all your imagination?"

"That's what the head-shrinkers tell me. I lost a week.
Seven days. They tell me I rented an apartment all right,
but I didn't put her in it because there never was any
Freyda. We didn't tear each other apart because there
was only me up there all the time. Alone. She wasn't a
crazy, mauling bitch who used to say: "Sigma, darling . . ."

"Say what?"

"You heard me. 'Sigma, darling.' That's how she said
good-by. 'Sigma, darling.' That's what she said on the
last day. With a crazy glitter in her virgin eyes. Told me
it was no good between us. That she'd phoned Liz and
told her all about it and was walking out. 'Sigma, darling,'
she said and started for the door."

"She told Liz? Told your wife?"

Bacon nodded. "I grabbed her and dragged her away
from the door. I locked the door and phoned Liz. That
tiger was tearing at me all the time. I got Liz on the
horn and it was true. Liz was packing. I hung that phone
up on that bitch's head. I was wild. I tore her clothes off.

I dragged her into the bedroom and threw her down and choked her. Christ! How I strangled her . . ."

After a pause, I asked: "Liz?"

"They were pounding on the door outside," Bacon went on. "I knew she was dead. She had to be dead. I went and opened the door. There were six million cops and six million honest johns still squawking about the screaming. I thought to myself: 'Why, this is just like the show you do every week. Play it like the script.' I said to them: 'Come on in and join the murder.'" He broke off.

"Was she dead . . . Freyda?"

"There was no murder," he said slowly. "There was no Freyda. That apartment was ten floors up in the Kingston Hotel. There wasn't any fire escape. There was only the front door jammed with cops and squares. And there was no one in the apartment but a crazy guy—naked, sweating and swearing. Me."

"She was gone? Where? How? It doesn't make sense."

He shook his head and stared at the table in sullen confusion. After a long pause he continued. "There was nothing left from Freyda but a crazy souvenir. It must have busted off in the fight we had—the fight everybody said was imaginary. It was the dial of her watch."

"What was crazy about it?"

"It was numbered from two to twenty-four by twos. Two, four, six, eight, ten . . . and so on."

"Maybe it was a foreign watch. Europeans use the twenty-four hour system. I mean, noon is twelve and one o'clock is thirteen and—"

"Don't overwhelm me," Bacon interrupted wearily. "I was in the army. I know all about that. But I've never seen a clock-face like that used for it. No one has. It was out of this world. I mean that literally."

"Yes? How?"

"I met her again."

"Freyda?"

He nodded. "I met her in Coney Island again, hanging around the roller coaster. I was no fool. I went looking for her and I found her."

"Beat up?"

"Not a mark on her. Fresh and virgin all over again, though it was only a couple of weeks later. There she was, the Black Widow Spider, smelling the flies as they came staggering off the roller coaster. I went up behind her and I grabbed her. I pulled her around into the alley between the freak tents and I said: 'Let out one peep and you're dead for sure this time.' "

"Did she fight?"

"No," he said. "She was loving it. She looked like she just found a million bucks. That glitter in her eyes . . ."

"I don't understand."

"*I* did when I looked at her. . . . When I looked into that virgin face, happy and smiling because I was screaming at her. I said: 'The cops swear nobody was in the apartment but me. The talk-doctors swear nobody was ever in the apartment but me. That put you into my imagination and *that* put *me* into the psycho ward for a week.' I said: 'But I know how you got out and I know where you went.' "

Bacon stopped and looked hard at me. I looked hard at him.

"How drunk are you?" he asked.

"Drunk enough to believe anything."

"She went out through time," Bacon said. "Understand? Through time. To another time. To the future. She melted and dissolved right out."

"What? Time travel? I'm not drunk enough to believe that."

"Time travel." He nodded. "That's why she had that watch—some kind of time machine. That's how she got herself patched up so fast. She could have stayed up there for a year and then come right back to Now or two weeks after Now. And that's why she said 'Sigma, darling.' It's how they talk up there."

"Now wait a minute, Eddie—"

"And that's why she wanted to come so close to getting herself killed."

"But that doesn't make sense. She wanted you to knock her around?"

"I told you. She loved it. They all love it. They come back here, the bastards, like we go to Coney Island. They don't come back to explore or study or any of that science-fiction crap. Our time's an amusement park for them, that's all. Like the roller coaster."

"How do you mean, the roller coaster?"

"Passion. Emotion. Screams and shrieks. Loving and hating and tearing and killing. That's their roller coaster. That's how they get their kicks. It must be forgotten up there in the future, like we've forgotten how it is to be chased by a dinosaur. So they come back here for it. This is the Stone Age for them."

"But—"

"All that stuff about the sudden up-swing in crime and violence and rape. It isn't us. We're no worse than we ever were. It's them. They came back here. They goad us. They needle us. They stick pins in us until we blow our tops and give their glands a roller coaster ride."

"And Liz?" I asked. "Did she believe this?"

He shook his head. "She never gave me a chance to tell her."

"I hear she kicked up quite a fuss."

"Yeah. Six beautiful feet of Irish rage. She took my gun off the study wall—the one I packed when I was with Patton. If it'd been loaded that wouldn't have been any make-believe murder."

"So I heard, Eddie. Where's Liz now?"

"Doing a burn in her old apartment."

"Where's that?"

"Ten-ten Park."

"Mrs. Elizabeth Bacon?"

"Not after Bacon got D.T.'s nailed to the name in the papers. She's using her maiden name."

"Oh, yes. Elizabeth Noyes, isn't it?"

"Noyes? Where the hell did you get that? No. Elizabeth Gorman." He yelled: "Chris! What is this—a desert?"

I looked at my time-meter. The hand was halfway from twelve to fourteen. That gave me eleven days more before I had to go back up. Just enough time to work Liz Gorman for some action. The gun sounded real promising. Freyda was right. It was a good lead. I got up from the table.

"Have to be going now, Eddie," I said. "Sigma, pal."

✳

Oddy and Id

THIS IS THE STORY OF A MONSTER.

They named him Odysseus Gaul in honor of Papa's favorite hero, and over Mama's desperate objections; but he was known as Oddy from the age of one.

The first year of life is an egotistic craving for warmth and security. Oddy was not likely to have much of that when he was born, for Papa's real estate business was bankrupt, and Mama was thinking of divorce. But an unexpected decision by United Radiation to build a plant in the town made Papa wealthy, and Mama fell in love with him all over again. So Oddy had warmth and security.

The second year of life is a timid exploration. Oddy crawled and explored. When he reached for the crimson coils inside the nonobjective fireplace, an unexpected short-circuit saved him from a burn. When he fell out the third floor window, it was into the grass filled hopper of the Mechano-Gardener. When he teased the Phoebus Cat, it slipped as it snapped at his face, and the brilliant fangs clicked harmlessly over his ear.

"Animals love Oddy," Mama said. "They only pretend to bite."

Oddy wanted to be loved, so everybody loved Oddy. He was petted, pampered and spoiled through pre-school age. Shopkeepers presented him with largess, and acquaintances showered him with gifts. Of sodas, candy, tarts, chrystons, bobble-trucks, freezies and various other comestibles, Oddy consumed enough for an entire kindergarten. He was never sick.

"Takes after his father," Papa said. "Good stock."

Family legends grew about Oddy's luck. . . . How a perfect stranger mistook him for his own child just as Oddy was about to amble into the Electronic Circus, and delayed him long enough to save him from the disastrous explosion of '98. . . . How a forgotten library book rescued him from the Rocket Crash of '99. . . . How a multitude of odd incidents saved him from a multitude of assorted catastrophes. No one realized he was a monster . . . yet.

At eighteen, he was a nice looking boy with seal-brown hair, warm brown eyes, and a wide grin that showed even white teeth. He was strong, healthy, intelligent. He was completely uninhibited in his quiet, relaxed way. He had charm. He was happy. So far, his monstrous evil had only affected the little Town Unit where he was born and raised.

He came to Harvard from a Progressive School, so when one of his many new friends popped into the dormitory room and said: "Hey Oddy, come down to the Quad and kick a ball around." Oddy answered: "I don't know how, Ben."

"Don't know how?" Ben tucked the football under his arm and dragged Oddy with him. "Where you been, laddie?"

"They didn't think much of football back home," Oddy grinned. "Said it was old fashioned. We were strictly Huxley-Hob."

"Huxley-Hob! That's for eggheads," Ben said. "Football is still the big game. You want to be famous? You got to be on that gridiron on TV every Saturday."

"So I've noticed, Ben. Show me."

Ben showed Oddy, carefully and with patience. Oddy took the lesson seriously and industriously. His third punt was caught by a freakish gust of wind, travelled seventy yards through the air, and burst through the third floor window of Proctor Charley (Gravy-Train) Stuart. Stuart took one look out the window and had Oddy down to Soldier Stadium in half an hour. Three Saturdays later, the headlines read: Oddy Gaul 57—Army 0.

"Snell and Rumination!" Coach Hig Clayton swore. "How does he do it? There's nothing sensational about that kid. He's just average. But when he runs they fall down chasing him. When he kicks, they fumble. When they fumble, he recovers."

"He's a negative player," Gravy-Train answered. "He lets you make the mistakes and then he cashes in."

They were both wrong. Oddy Gaul was a monster.

With his choice of any eligible young woman, Oddy Gaul went stag to the Observatory Prom, wandered into a darkroom by mistake, and discovered a girl in a smock bending over trays in the hideous green safe-light. She had cropped black hair, icy blue eyes, strong features, and a sensuous boyish figure. She ordered him out and Oddy fell in love with her . . . temporarily.

His friends howled with laughter when he told them. "Shades of Pygmalion, Oddy, don't you know about *her*? The girl is frigid. A statue. She loathes men. You're wasting your time."

But through the adroitness of her analyst, the girl turned a neurotic corner one week later and fell deeply in love with Oddy Gaul. It was sudden, devastating and enraptured for two months. Then just as Oddy began to cool, the girl had a relapse and everything ended on a friendly, convenient basis.

So far only minor events made up the response to Oddy's luck, but the shock-wave of reaction was spreading. In September of his Sophomore year, Oddy competed for the Political Economy Medal with a thesis entitled: "Causes of Mutiny." The striking similarity of his paper to the Astraean Mutiny that broke out the day his paper was entered won him the prize.

In October, Oddy contributed twenty dollars to a pool organized by a crack-pot classmate for speculating on the Exchange according to "Stock Market Trends," an ancient superstition. The prophet's calculations were ridiculous, but a sharp panic nearly ruined the Exchange as it quadrupled the pool. Oddy made one hundred dollars.

And so it went . . . worse and worse. The monster.

Now a monster can get away with a lot when he's studying speculative philosophy where causation is rooted in history and the Present is devoted to statistical analysis of the Past; but the living sciences are bulldogs with their teeth clamped on the phenomena of Now. So it was Jesse Migg, physiologist and spectral physicist, who first trapped the monster . . . and he thought he'd found an angel.

Old Jess was one of the Sights. In the first place he was young . . . not over forty. He was a malignant knife of a man, an albino, pink-eyed, bald, pointed-nosed and brilliant. He affected twentieth century clothes and twentieth century vices . . . tobacco and potation so C_2H_5OH. He never talked . . . He spat. He never walked . . . He scurried. And he was scurrying up and down the aisles of the laboratory of Tech I (General Survey of Spatial Mechanics—Required for All General Arts Students) when he ferreted out the monster.

One of the first experiments in the course was EMF Electrolysis. Elementary stuff. A U-Tube containing water was passed between the poles of a stock Remosant Magnet. After sufficient voltage was transmitted through the coils, you drew off Hydrogen and Oxygen in two-to-one ratio at the arms of the tube and related them to the voltage and the magnetic field.

Oddy ran his experiment earnestly, got the approved results, entered them in his lab book and then waited for the official check-off. Little Migg came hustling down the aisle, darted to Oddy and spat: "Finished?"

"Yes, sir."

Migg checked the book entries, glanced at the indicators at the ends of the tube, and stamped Oddy out with a sneer. It was only after Oddy was gone that he noticed the Remosant Magnet was obviously shorted. The wires were fused. There hadn't been any field to electrolyze the water.

"Hell and Damnation!" Migg grunted (he also affected twentieth century vituperation) and rolled a clumsy cigarette.

He checked off possibilities in his comptometer head. 1. Gaul cheated. 2. If so, with what apparatus did he portion out the H_2 and O_2? 3. Where did he get the pure gases? 4. Why did he do it? Honesty was easier. 5. He didn't cheat. 6. How did he get the right results? 7. How did he get *any* results?

Old Jess emptied the U-Tube, refilled it with water and ran off the experiment himself. He too got the correct result without a magnet.

"Christ on a Raft!" he swore, unimpressed by the miracle, and infuriated by the mystery. He snooped, darting about like a hungry bat. After four hours he discovered that the steel bench supports were picking up a charge from the Greeson Coils in the basement and had thrown just enough field to make everything come out right.

"Coincidence," Migg spat. But he was not convinced.

Two weeks later, in Elementary Fission Analysis, Oddy completed his afternoon's work with a careful listing of resultant isotopes from selenium to lanthanum. The only trouble, Migg discovered, was that there had been a mistake in the stock issued to Oddy. He hadn't received any U^{235} for neutron bombardment. His sample had been a left-over from a Stefan-Boltzmann black-body demonstration.

"God in Heaven!" Migg swore, and double-checked. Then he triple-checked. When he found the answer—a remarkable coincidence involving improperly cleaned apparatus and a defective cloud-chamber—he swore further. He also did some intensive thinking.

"There are accident prones," Migg snarled at the reflection in his Self-Analysis Mirror. "How about Good Luck prones? Horse Manure!"

But he was a bulldog with his teeth sunk in phenomena. He tested Oddy Gaul. He hovered over him in the laboratory, cackling with infuriated glee as Oddy completed experiment after experiment with defective equipment. When Oddy successfully completed the Rutherford Classic—getting $_8O^{17}$ after exposing nitrogen to alpha radiation, but in this case without the use of nitrogen or alpha radiation—Migg actually clapped him on the back in delight. Then the little man investigated and found the logical, improbable chain of coincidences that explained it.

He devoted his spare time to a check-back on Oddy's career at Harvard. He had a two hour conference with a lady astronomer's faculty analyst, and a ten minute talk with Hig Clayton and Gravy-Train Stuart. He rooted out the Exchange Pool, the Political Economy Medal, and half a dozen other incidents that filled him with malignant joy. Then he cast off his twentieth century affectation, dressed himself properly in formal leotards, and entered the Faculty Club for the first time in a year.

A four-handed chess game on a transparent toroid board was in progress in the Diathermy Alcove. It had been in progress since Migg joined the faculty, and would probably not be finished before the end of the century. In fact, Johansen, playing Red, was already training his son to replace him in the likely event of his dying before the completion of the game.

As abrupt as ever, Migg marched up to the glowing board, sparkling with vari-colored pieces, and blurted: "What do you know about accidents?"

"Ah?" said Bellanby, *Philosopher in Res* at the University. "Good evening, Migg. Do you mean the accident of substance, or the accident of essence? If, on the other hand, your question implies—"

"No, no," Migg interrupted. "My apologies, Bellanby. Let me rephrase the question. Is there such a thing as Compulsion of Probability?"

Hrrdnikkisch completed his move and gave full attention to Migg, as did Johansen and Bellanby. Wilson continued to study the board. Since he was permitted one hour to make his move and would need it, Migg knew there would be ample time for the discussion.

"Compulthon of Probability?" Hrrdnikkisch lisped. "Not a new conthept, Migg. I recall a thurvey of the theme in 'The Integraph' Vol. LVIII, No. 9. The calculuth, if I am not mithtaken—"

"No," Migg interrupted again. "My respects, Signoid. I'm not interested in the mathematic of Probability, nor the philosophy. Let me put it this way. The Accident Prone has already been incorporated into the body of Psychoanalysis. Paton's Theorem of the Lease Neurotic Norm settled that. But I've discovered the obverse. I've discovered a Fortune Prone."

"Ah?" Johansen chuckled. "It's to be a joke. You wait and see, Signoid."

"No," answered Migg. "I'm perfectly serious. I've discovered a genuinely lucky man."

"He wins at cards?"

"He wins at everything. Accept this postulate for the moment. . . . I'll document it later. . . . There is a man who is lucky. He is a Fortune Prone. Whatever he desires, he receives. Whether he has the ability to achieve it or not, he receives it. If his desire is totally beyond the peak of his accomplishment, then the factors of chance, coincidence, hazard, accident . . . and so on, combine to produce his desired end."

"No." Bellanby shook his head. "Too far-fetched."

"I've worked it out empirically," Migg continued. "It's something like this. The future is a choice of mutually exclusive possibilities, one or other of which must be realized in terms of favorability of the events and number of the events. . . ."

"Yes, yes," interrupted Johansen. "The greater the number of favorable possibilities, the stronger the probability of an event maturing. This is elementary, Migg. Go on."

"I continue," Migg spat indignantly. "When we discuss Probability in terms of throwing dice, the predictions or odds are simple. There are only six mutually exclusive possibilities to each die. The favorability is easy to compute. Chance is reduced to simple odds-ratios. *But* when we discuss probability in terms of the Universe, we cannot encompass enough data to make a prediction. There are too many factors. Favorability cannot be ascertained."

"All thith ith true," Hrrdnikkisch said, "but what of your Fortune Prone?"

"I don't know how he does it . . . but merely by the intensity or mere existence of his desire, he can affect the favorability of possibilities. By wanting, he can turn possibility into probability, and probability into certainty."

"Ridiculous," Bellanby snapped. "You claim there's a man far-sighted and far-reaching enough to do this?"

"Nothing of the sort. He doesn't know what he's doing. He just thinks he's lucky, if he thinks about it at all. Let us say he wants . . . Oh . . . Name anything."

"Heroin," Bellanby said.

"What's that?" Johansen inquired.

"A morphine derivative," Hrrdnikkisch explained.

"Formerly manufactured and thold to narcotic addictth."

"Heroin," Migg said. "Excellent. Say my man desires heroin, an antique narcotic no longer in existence. Very good. His desire would compel this sequence of possible but improbable events: A chemist in Australia, fumbling through a new organic synthesis, will accidentally and unwittingly prepare six ounces of heroin. Four ounces will be discarded, but through a logical mistake two ounces will be preserved. A further coincidence will ship it to this country and this city, wrapped as powdered sugar in a plastic ball; where the final accident will serve it to my man in a restaurant which he is visiting for the first time on an impulse. . . ."

"La-La-La!" said Hrrdnikkisch. "Thith shuffling of hithtory. Thith fluctuation of inthident and pothibility? All achieved without the knowledge but with the dethire of a man?"

"Yes. Precisely my point," Migg snarled. "I don't know how he does it, but he turns possibility into certianty. And since almost anything is possible, he is capable of accomplishing almost anything. He is Godlike but not a god because he does this without consciousness. He is an angel."

"Who is this angel?" Johansen asked.

And Migg told them all about Oddy Gaul.

"But how does he do it?" Bellanby persisted. "How does he do it?"

"I don't know," Migg repeated again. "Tell me how Espers do it."

"What!" Bellanby exclaimed. "Are you prepared to deny the telepathic pattern of thought? Do you—"

"I do nothing of the sort. I merely illustrate one possible explanation. Man produces events. The threatening War of Resources may be thought to be a result of the natural exhaustion of terran resources. We know it is not. It is a result of centuries of thriftless waste by man. Natural phenomena are less often produced by nature and more often produced by man."

"And?"

"Who knows? Gaul is producing phenomena. Perhaps he's unconsciously broadcasting on a telepathic waveband. Broadcasting and getting results. He wants Heroin. The broadcast goes out—"

"But Espers can't pick up any telepathic pattern further than the horizon. It's direct wave transmission. Even large objects cannot be penetrated. A building, say, or a—"

"I'm not saying this is on the Esper level," Migg shouted. "I'm trying to imagine something bigger. Something tremendous. He wants heroin. His broadcast goes out to the world. All men unconsciously fall into a pattern of activity which will produce that heroin as quickly as possible. That Austrian chemist—"

"No. Australian."

"That Australian chemist may have been debating between half a dozen different syntheses. Five of them could never have produced heroin; but Gaul's impulse made him select the sixth."

"And if he did not anyway?"

"Then who knows what parallel chains were also started? A boy playing Robin Hood in Montreal is impelled to explore an abandoned cabin where he finds the drug, hidden there centuries ago by smugglers. A woman in California collects old apothecary jars. She finds a pound of heroin. A child in Berlin, playing with a defective Radar-Chem Set, manufactures it. Name the most improbable sequence of events, and Gaul can bring it about, logically and certainly. I tell you, that boy is an angel!"

And he produced his documented evidence and convinced them.

It was then that four scholars of various but indisputable intellects elected themselves an executive committee for Fate and took Oddy Gaul in hand. To understand what they attempted to do, you must first understand the situation the world found itself in during that particular era.

It is a known fact that all wars are founded in economic conflict, or to put it another way, a trial by arms is merely the last battle of an economic war. In the pre-Christian centuries, the Punic Wars were the final outcome of a financial struggle between Rome and Carthage for economic control of the Mediterranean. Three thousand years later, the impending War of Resources loomed as the finale of a struggle between the two Independent Welfare States controlling most of the known economic world.

What petroleum oil was to the Twentieth century, FO (the nickname for Fissionable Ore) was to the Thirtieth; and the situation was peculiarly similar to the Asia Minor crisis that ultimately wrecked the United Nations a thousand years before. Triton, a backward semibarbaric satellite, previously unwanted and ignored, had suddenly discovered it possessed enormous resources of FO. Financially and technologically incapable of self-development, Triton was peddling concessions to both Welfare States.

The difference between a Welfare State and a Benevolent Despot is slight. In times of crisis, either can be traduced by the sincerest motives into the most abominable conduct. Both the Comity of Nations (bitterly nicknamed "The Con Men" by Der Realpolitik aus Terra) and Der Realpolitik aus Terra (sardonically called "The Rats" by the Comity of Nations) were desperately in need of natural resources, meaning FO. They were bidding against each other hysterically, and elbowing each other with sharp skirmishes at outposts. Their sole concern was the protection of their citizens. From the best of motives they were preparing to cut each other's throat.

Had this been the issue before the citizens of both Welfare States, some compromise might have been reached; but Triton, intoxicated as a schoolboy with a newfound prominence and power, confused issues by raising a religious issue and reviving a Holy War which the Family of Planets had long forgotten. Assistance in their Holy War (involving the extermination of a harmless and rather unimportant sect called the Quakers) was one of the conditions of sale. This, both the Comity of Nations and Der Realpolitik aus Terra were prepared to swallow with or without private reservations, but it could not be admitted to their citizens.

And so, camouflaged by the burning issues of Rights of Minority Sects, Priority of Pioneering, Freedom of Religion, Historical Rights to Triton v. Possession in Fact, etc., the two Houses of the Family of Planets feinted, parried, riposted and slowly closed, like fencers on the strip, for the final sortie which meant ruin for both.

All this the four men discussed through three interminable meetings.

"Look here," Migg complained toward the close of the third consultation. "You theoreticians have already turned nine manhours into carbonic acid with ridiculous dissensions . . ."

Bellanby nodded, smiling. "It's as I've always said, Migg. Every man nurses the secret belief that were he

God he could do the job much better. We're just learning how difficult it is."

"Not God," Hrrdnikkisch said, "but hith Prime Min- ithterth. Gaul will be God."

Johansen winced. "I don't like that talk," he said. "I happen to be a religious man."

"You?" Bellanby exclaimed in surprise. "A Colloid- Therapeutist?"

"I happen to be a religious man," Johansen repeated stubbornly.

"But the boy hath the power of the miracle," Hrrdnik- kisch protested. "When he hath been taught to know what he doth, he will be a God."

"This is pointless," Migg rapped out. "We have spent three sessions in piffling discussion. I have heard three opposed views re Mr. Odysseus Gaul. Although all are agreed he must be used as a tool, none can agree on the work to which the tool must be set. Bellanby prattles about an Ideal Intellectual Anarchy, Johansen preaches about a Soviet of God, and Hrrdnikkisch has wasted two hours postulating and destroying his own theorems. . . ."

"Really, Migg . . ." Hrrdnikkisch began. Migg waved his hand.

"Permit me," Migg continued malevolently, "to reduce this discussion to the kindergarten level. First things first, gentlemen. Before attempting to reach cosmic agreement we must make sure there is a cosmos left for us to agree upon. I refer to the impending war. . . .

"Our program, as I see it, must be simple and di- rect. It is the education of a God or, if Johansen pro- tests, of an angel. Fortunately Gaul is an estimable young man of kindly, honest disposition. I shudder to think what he might have done had he been inherently vicious."

"Or what he might do once he learns what he can do," muttered Bellanby.

"Precisely. We must begin a careful and rigorous ethi- cal education of the boy, but we haven't enough time. We can't educate first, and then explain the truth when he's safe. We must forestall the war. We need a short- cut."

"All right," Johansen said. "What do you suggest?"

"Dazzlement," Migg spat. "Enchantment."

"Enchantment?" Hrrdnikkisch chuckled. "A new thi- enth, Migg?"

"Why do you think I selected you three of all people for this secret?" Migg snorted. "For your intellects? Nonsense! I can think you all under the table. No. I selected you, gentlemen, for your charm."

"It's an insult," Bellanby grinned, "and yet I'm flattered."

"Gaul is nineteen," Migg went on. "He is at the age when undergraduates are most susceptible to hero-worship. I want you gentlemen to charm him. You are not the first brains of the University, but you are the first heroes."

"I altho am inthulted and flattered," said Hrrdnikkisch.

"I want you to charm him, dazzle him, inspire him with affection and awe . . . as you've done with countless classes of undergraduates."

"Aha!" said Johansen. "The chocolate around the pill."

"Exactly. When he's enchanted, you will make him want to stop the war . . . and then tell him how he can stop it. That will give us breathing space to continue his education. By the time he outgrows his respect for you he will have a sound ethical foundation on which to build. He'll be safe."

"And you, Migg?" Bellanby inquired. "What part do you play?"

"Now? None," Migg snarled. "I have no charm, gentlemen. I come later. When he outgrows his respect for you, he'll begin to acquire respect for me."

All of which was frightfully conceited but perfectly true.

And as events slowly marched toward the final crisis, Oddy Gaul was carefully and quickly enchanted. Bellanby invited him to the twenty foot crystal globe atop his house . . . the famous hen-roost to which only the favored few were invited. There, Oddy Gaul sun-bathed and admired the philosopher's magnificent iron-hard condition at seventy-three. Admiring Bellanby's muscles, it was only natural for him to admire Bellanby's ideas. He returned often to sun-bathe, worship the great man, and absorb ethical concepts.

Meanwhile, Hrrdnikkisch took over Oddy's evenings. With the mathematician, who puffed and lisped like some flamboyant character out of Rabelais, Oddy was carried to the dizzy heights of the *haute cuisine* and the complete pagan life. Together they ate and drank incredible foods and liquids and pursued incredible women until Oddy returned to his room each night intoxicated with the magic of the senses and the riotous color of the great Hrrdnikkisch's glittering ideas.

And occasionally . . . not too often, he would find Papa Johansen waiting for him, and then would come the long quiet talks through the small hours when young men search for the harmonics of life and the meaning of entity. And there was Johansen for Oddy to model himself after . . . a glowing embodiment of Spiritual Good . . . a living example of Faith in God and Ethical Sanity.

The climax came on March 15 . . . The Ides of March, and they should have taken the date as a sign. After dinner with his three heroes at the Faculty Club, Oddy was ushered into the Foto-Library by the three great men where they were joined, quite casually, by Jesse Migg. There passed a few moments of uneasy tension until Migg made a sign, and Bellanby began.

"Oddy," he said, "have you ever had the fantasy that some day you might wake up and discover you were a King?"

Oddy blushed.

"I see you have. You know, every man has entertained that dream. It's called the Mignon Complex. The usual pattern is: You learn your parents have only adopted you, and that you are actually and rightfully the King of . . . of . . ."

"Baratraria," said Hrrdnikkisch, who had made a study of Stone Age Fiction.

"Yes, sir," Oddy muttered. "I've had that dream."

"Well," Bellanby said quietly, "it's come true. You are a King."

Oddy stared while they explained and explained and explained. First, as a college boy, he was wary and suspicious of a joke. Then, as an idolator, he was almost persuaded by the men he most admired. And finally, as a human animal, he was swept away by the exaltation of security. Not power, not glory, not wealth thrilled him, but security alone. Later he might come to enjoy the trimmings, but now he was released from fear. He need never worry again.

"Yes," exclaimed Oddy. "Yes, yes, yes! I understand. I understand what you want me to do." He surged up excitedly from his chair and circled the illuminated walls, trembling with joy. Then he stopped and turned.

"And I'm grateful," he said. "Grateful to all of you for what you've been trying to do. It would have been shame-

ful if I'd been selfish . . . or mean. . . . Trying to use
this for myself. But you've shown me the way. It's to be
used for good. Always!"

Johansen nodded happily.

"I'll always listen to you," Oddy went on. "I don't want
to make any mistakes. Ever!" He paused and blushed
again. "That dream about being a king . . . I had that
when I was a kid. But here at the school I've had something bigger. I used to wonder what would happen if I
was the one man who could run the world. I used to
dream about the kind, generous things I'd do. . . ."

"Yes," said Bellanby. "We know, Oddy. We've all had
that dream too. Every man does."

"But it isn't a dream any more," Oddy laughed. "It's
reality. I can do it. I can make it happen."

"Start with the war," Migg said sourly.

"Of course," said Oddy. "The war first; but then we'll
go on from there, won't we? I'll make sure the war never
starts, but then we'll do big things . . . great things!
Just the five of us in private. Nobody'll know about us.
We'll be ordinary people, but we'll make life wonderful for
everybody. If I'm an angel . . . like you say . . . then I'll
spread heaven around me as far as I can reach."

"But start with the war," Migg repeated.

"The war is the first disaster that must be averted,
Oddy," Bellanby said. "If you don't want this disaster to
happen, it will never happen."

"And you want to prevent that tragedy, don't you?"
said Johansen.

"Yes," answered Oddy. "I do."

On March 20, the war broke. The Comity of Nations
and Der Realpolitik aus Terra mobilized and struck. While
blow followed shattering counter-blow, Oddy Gaul was
commissioned Subaltern in a line regiment, but gazetted
to Intelligence on May 3. On June 24 he was appointed
A.D.C. to the Joint Forces Council meeting in the ruins
of what had been Australia. On July 11, he was brevetted
to command of the wrecked Space Force, being jumped
1,789 grades over regular officers. On September 19
he assumed supreme command in the Battle of the Parsec
and won the victory that ended the disastrous solar an-
nihilation called the Six Month War.

On September 23, Oddy Gaul made the astonishing
Peace Offer that was accepted by the remnants of both
Welfare States. It required the scrapping of antagonistic

economic theories, and amounted to the virtual aban-
donment of all economic theory with an amalgamation
of both States into a Solar Society. On January 1, Oddy
Gaul, by unanimous acclaim, was elected Solon of the
Solar Society in perpetuity.

And today . . . still youthful, still vigorous, still handsome, still sincere, idealistic, charitable, kindly and sym-
pathetic, he lives in the Solar Palace. He is unmarried
but a mighty lover; uninhibited, but a charming host and
devoted friend; democratic, but the feudal overload of a
bankrupt Family of Planets that suffers misgovernment,
oppression, poverty and confusion with a cheerful joy that
sings nothing but Hosannahs to the glory of Oddy Gaul.

In a last moment of clarity, Jesse Migg communicated
his desolate summation of the situation to his friends in
the Faculty Club. This was shortly before they made the
trip to join Oddy in the palace as his confidential and
valued advisers.

"We were fools," Migg said bitterly. "We should have
killed him. He isn't an angel. He's a monster. Civilization
and culture . . . philosophy and ethics . . . those were
only masks Oddy put on; masks that covered the primitive impulses of his subconscious mind."

"You mean Oddy was not sincere?" Johansen asked
heavily. "He wanted this wreckage . . . this ruin?"

"Certainly he was sincere . . . consciously. He still is.
He thinks he desires nothing but the most good for the
most men. He's honest, kind and generous . . . but only
consciously."

"Ah! The Id!" said Hrrdnikkisch with an explosion of
breath as though he had been punched in the stomach.

"You understand, Signoid? I see you do. Gentlemen, we
were imbeciles. We made the mistake of assuming that
Oddy would have conscious control of his power. He
does not. The control was and still is below the thinking,
reasoning level. The control lies in Oddy's Id . . . in that
deep unconscious reservoir of primordial selfishness that
lies within every man."

"Then he wanted the war," Bellanby said.

"His Id wanted the war, Bellanby. It was the quickest
route to what his Id desires . . . to be Lord of the Universe and loved by the Universe . . . and his Id controls
the Power. All of us have that selfish, egocentric Id within us, perpetually searching for satisfaction, timeless, immortal, knowing no logic, no values, no good and evil, no

morality; and that is what controls the power in Oddy. He will always win, not what he's been educated to desire but what his Id desires. It's the inescapable conflict that may be the doom of our system."

"But we'll be there to advise him . . . counsel him . . . guide him," Bellanby protested. "He asked us to come."

"And he'll listen to our advice like the good child that he is," Migg answered, "agreeing with us, trying to make a heaven for everybody while his Id will be making a hell for everybody. Oddy isn't unique. We all suffer from the same conflict . . . but Oddy has the power."

"What can we do?" Johansen groaned. "What can we do?"

"I don't know." Migg bit his lip, then bobbed his head to Papa Johansen in what amounted to apology for him. "Johansen," he said, "you were right. There must be a God, if only because there must be an opposite to Oddy Gaul who was most assuredly invented by the Devil."

But that was Jesse Migg's last sane statement. Now, of course, he adores Gaul the Glorious, Gaul the Gauleiter, Gaul the God Eternal who has achieved the savage, self-fish satisfaction for which all of us unconsciously yearn from birth, but which only Oddy Gaul has won.

✳

The Starcomber

TAKE TWO PARTS OF BEELZEBUB, TWO OF ISRAFEL, one of Monte Cristo, one of Cyrano, mix violently, season with mystery and you have Mr. Solon Aquila. He is tall, gaunt, sprightly in manner, bitter in expression, and when he laughs his dark eyes turn into wounds. His occupation is unknown. He is wealthy without visible means of support. He is seen everywhere and understood nowhere. There is something odd about his life.

This is what's odd about Mr. Aquila, and you can make what you will of it. When he walks he is never forced to wait on a traffic signal. When he desires to ride there is always a vacant taxi on hand. When he bustles into his hotel an elevator always happens to be waiting. When he enters a store, a salesclerk is always free to serve him. There always happens to be a table available for Mr. Aquila in restaurants. There are always last-minute ticket returns when he craves entertainment at sold-out shows.

You can question waiters, hack drivers, elevator girls, salesmen, box-office men. There is no conspiracy. Mr. Aquila does not bribe or blackmail for these petty conveniences. In any case, it would not be possible for him to bribe or blackmail the automatic clock that governs the city traffic signal system. These things, which make life so convenient for him, simply happen. Mr. Solon Aquila is never disappointed. Presently we shall hear about his first disappointment and see what it led to.

Mr. Aquila has been seen fraternizing in low saloons, in middle saloons, in high saloons. He has been met in bagnois, at coronations, executions, circuses, magistrate's courts and handbook offices. He has been known to buy antique cars, historic jewels, incunabula, pornography, chemicals, porro prisms, polo ponies and full-choke shotguns.

"HimmelHerrGottSeiDank! I'm crazy, man, crazy. Eclectic, by God," he told a flabbergasted department store president. "The Weltmann type, nicht wahr? My ideal: Goethe. Tout le monde. God damn."

He spoke a spectacular tongue of mixed metaphors and meanings. Dozens of languages and dialects came out in machine-gun bursts. Apparently he also lied *ad libitum*.

"Sacré bleu. Jeez!" he was heard to say once. "Aquila from the Latin. Means aquiline. O tempora O mores. Speech by Cicero. My ancestor."

And another time: "My idol: Kipling. Took my name from him. Aquila, one of his heroes. God damn. Greatest Negro writer since *Uncle Tom's Cabin*."

On the morning that Mr. Solon Aquila was stunned by his first disappointment, he bustled into the atelier of Lagan & Derelict, dealers in paintings, sculpture and rare objects of art. It was his intention to buy a painting. Mr. James Derelict knew Aquila as a client. Aquila had already purchased a Frederic Remington and a Winslow Homer some time ago when, by another odd coincidence, he had bounced into the Madison Avenue shop one minute after the coveted paintings went up for sale. Mr. Derelict had also seen Mr. Aquila boat a prize striper at Montauk.

"Bon soir, bel esprit, God damn, Jimmy," Mr. Aquila said. He was on first name terms with everyone. "Here's a cool day for color, oui! Cool. Slang. I have in me to buy a picture."

"Good morning, Mr. Aquila," Derelict answered. He had the seamed face of a cardsharp, but his blue eyes were honest and his smile was disarming. However at this moment his smile seemed strained, as though the volatile appearance of Aquila had unnerved him.

"I'm in the mood for your man, by Jeez," Aquila said, rapidly opening cases, fingering ivories and tasting the porcelains. "What's his name, my old? Artist like Bosch. Like Heinrich Kley. You handle him, parbleu, exclusive. O si sic omnia, by Zeus!"

"Jeffrey Halsyon?" Derelict asked timidly.

"Oeil de boeuf!" Aquila cried. "What a memory. Chryselephantine. Exactly the artist I want. He is my favorite. A monochrome, preferably. A small Jeffrey Halsyon for Aquila, bitte. Wrap her up."

"I wouldn't have believed it," Derelict muttered.

"Ah! Ah-ha? This is not 100 proof guaranteed Ming," Mr. Aquila exclaimed brandishing an exquisite vase. "Caveat emptor, by damn. Well, Jimmy? I snap my fingers. No Halsyons in stock, old faithful?"

"It's extremely odd, Mr. Aquila," Derelict seemed to struggle with himself. "Your coming in like this. A Halsyon monochrome arrived not five minutes ago."

"You see? Tempo ist Richtung. Well?"

"I'd rather not show it to you. For personal reasons, Mr. Aquila."

"HimmelHerrGott! Pourquoi? She's bespoke?"

"N-no, sir. Not for *my* personal reasons. For *your* personal reasons."

"Oh? God damn. Explain myself to me."

"Anyway, it isn't for sale, Mr. Aquila. It can't be sold."

"For why not? Speak, old fish and chips."

"I can't say, Mr. Aquila."

"Zut alors! Must I judo your arm, Jimmy? You can't show. You can't sell. Me, internally, I have pressurized myself for a Jeffrey Halsyon. My favorite. God damn. Show me the Halsyon or sic transit gloria mundi. You hear me, Jimmy?"

Derelict hesitated, then shrugged. "Very well, Mr. Aquila. I'll show you."

Derelict led Aquila past cases of china and silver, past lacquer and bronzes and suits of shimmering armor to the gallery in the rear of the shop where dozens of paintings hung on the gray velour walls, glowing under warm spotlights. He opened a drawer in a Goddard breakfront and took out an envelope. On the envelope was printed BABYLON INSTITUTE. From the envelope Derelict withdrew a dollar bill and handed it to Mr. Aquila.

"Jeffrey Halsyon's latest," he said.

With a fine pen and carbon ink, a cunning hand had drawn another portrait over the face of George Washington on the dollar bill. It was a hateful, diabolic face set in a hellish background. It was a face to strike terror, in a scene to inspire loathing. The face was a portrait of Mr. Aquila.

"God damn," Mr. Aquila said.

"You see, sir? I didn't want to hurt your feelings."

"Now I must own him, big boy." Mr. Aquila appeared to be fascinated by the portrait. "Is she accident or for purpose? Does Halsyon know myself? Ergo sum."

"Not to my knowledge, Mr. Aquila. But in any event I can't sell the drawing. It's evidence of a felony . . . mutilating United States currency. It must be destroyed."

"Never!" Mr. Aquila returned the drawing as though he feared the dealer would instantly set fire to it. "Never, Jimmy. Nevermore quoth the raven. God damn. Why does he draw on money, Halsyon? My picture, pfui. Criminal libels but n'importe. But pictures on money? Wasteful. Joci causa."

"He's insane, Mr. Aquila."

"No! Yes? Insane?" Aquila was shocked.

"Quite insane, sir. It's very sad. They've had to put him away. He spends his time drawing these pictures on money."

"God damn, mon ami. Who gives him money?"

"I do, Mr. Aquila; and his friends. Whenever we visit him he begs for money for his drawings."

"Le jour viendra, by Jeez! Why you don't give him paper for drawings, eh, my ancient of days?"

Derelict smiled sadly. "We tried that, sir. When we gave Jeff paper, he drew pictures of money."

"HimmelHerrGott! My favorite artist. In the looney bin. Eh bien. How in the holy hell am I to buy paintings from same if such be the case?"

"You won't, Mr. Aquila. I'm afraid no one will ever buy a Halsyon again. He's quite hopeless."

"Why does he jump his tracks, Jimmy?"

"They say its a withdrawal, Mr. Aquila. His success did it to him."

"Ah? Q.E.D. me, big boy, Translate."

"Well, sir, he's still a young man; in his thirties and very immature. When he became so very successful, he wasn't ready for it. He wasn't prepared for the responsibilities of his life and his career. That's what the doctors told me. So he turned his back on everything and withdrew into childhood."

"Ah? And the drawing on money?"

"They say that's his symbol of his return to childhood, Mr. Aquila. It proves he's too young to know what money is for."

"Ah? Oui. Ja. Astute, by crackey. And my portrait?"

"I can't explain that, Mr. Aquila, unless you have met him in the past and he remembers you somehow. Or it may be a coincidence."

"Hmmm. Perhaps. So. You know something, my attic of Greece? I am disappointed. Je n'oublierai jamais. I am most severely disappointed. God damn. No more Halsyons ever? Merde. My slogan. We must do something about Jeffrey Halsyon. I will not be disappointed. We must do something."

Mr. Solon Aquila nodded his head emphatically, took out a cigarette, took out a lighter, then paused, deep in thought. After a long moment, he nodded again, this time with decision, and did an astonishing thing. He returned the lighter to his pocket, took out another, glanced around quickly and lit it under Mr. Derelict's nose.

Mr. Derelict appeared not to notice. Mr. Derelict appeared, in one instant, to be frozen. Allowing the lighter to burn, Mr. Aquila placed it carefully on a ledge in front of the art dealer who stood before it without moving. The orange flame gleamed on his glassy eyeballs.

Aquila darted out into the shop, searched and found a rare Chinese crystal globe. He took it from its case, warmed it against his heart and peered into it. He mumbled. He nodded. He returned the globe to the case, went to the cashier's desk, took a pad and pencil and began ciphering in symbols that bore no relationship to any language or any graphology. He nodded again, tore up the sheet of paper and took out his wallet.

From the wallet he removed a dollar bill. He placed the bill on the glass counter, took an assortment of foun-

tain pens from his vest pocket, selected one and un-
screwed it. Carefully shielding his eyes, he allowed one
drop to fall from the pen point onto the bill. There was a
blinding flash of light. There was a humming vibration
that slowly died.

Mr. Aquila returned the pens to his pocket, carefully
picked up the bill by a corner and ran back into the picture gallery where the art dealer still stood staring glassily
at the orange flame. Aquila fluttered the bill before the
sightless eyes.

"Listen, my ancient," Aquila whispered. "You will visit
Jeffrey Halsyon this afternoon. N'est-ce pas? You will
give him this very own coin of the realm when he asks
for drawing materials. Eh? God damn." He removed Mr.
Derelict's wallet from his pocket, placed the bill inside
and returned the wallet.

"And this is why you make the visit," Aquila continued. "It is because you have had an inspiration from
le Diable Boiteux. Nolens volens, the lame devil has inspired you with a plan for healing Jeffrey Halsyon. God
damn. You will show him samples of his great art of the
past to bring him to his senses. Memory is the all-mother.
HimmelHerrGott. You hear me, big boy? You do what
I say. Go today and devil take the hindmost."

Mr. Aquila picked up the burning lighter, lit his cigarette and permitted the flame to go out. As he did so, he
said: "No, my holy of holies! Jeffrey Halsyon is too great
an artist to languish in durance vile. He must be returned
to this world. He must be returned to me. È sempre
l'ora. I will not be disappointed. You hear me, Jimmy? I
will not!"

"Perhaps there's hope, Mr. Aquila," James Derelict said.
"Something's just occurred to me while you were talking
. . . a way to bring Jeff back to sanity. I'm going to try
it this afternoon."

As he drew the face of the Faraway Fiend over George
Washington's portrait on a bill, Jeffrey Halsyon dictated
his autobiography to nobody.

"Like Cellini," he recited. "Line and literature simultaneously. Hand in hand, although all art is one art, holy
brothers in barbiturate, near ones and dear ones in nem-
butal. Very well. I commence: I was born. I am dead.
Baby wants a dollar. No—"

He arose from the padded floor and raged from padded

wall to padded wall, envisioning anger as a deep purple
fury running into the pale lavenders of recrimination by
the magic of his brushwork, his chiaroscuro, by the clever
blending of oil, pigment, light and the stolen genius of
Jeffrey Halsyon torn from him by the Faraway Fiend
whose hideous face—

"Begin anew," he muttered. "We darken the highlights.
Start with the underpainting . . ." He squatted on the
floor again, picked up the quill drawing pen whose point
was warranted harmless, dipped it into carbon ink whose
contents were warranted poisonless, and applied himself
to the monstrous face of the Faraway Fiend which was
replacing the first President on the dollar.

"I was born," he dictated to space while his cunning
hand wrought beauty and horror on the banknote paper.
"I had peace. I had hope. I had art. I had peace. Mama.
Papa. Kin I have a glass of water? Oooo! There was a
big bad bogey man who gave me a bad look; and now
baby's afraid. Mama! Baby wantsa make pretty pictures
onna pretty paper for Mama and Papa. Look, Mama. Baby
makin' a picture of the bad bogey man with a mean
look, a black look with his black eyes like pools of hell,
like cold fires of terror, like faraway fiends from faraway
fears— Who's that!"

The cell door unbolted. Halsyon leaped into a corner
and cowered, naked and squalling, as the door was
opened for the Faraway Fiend to enter. But it was only
the medicine man in his white jacket and a stranger
man in black suit, black homburg, carrying a black portfolio with the initials J. D. lettered on it in a bastard gold
Gothic with ludricous overtones of Goudy and Baskerville.

"Well, Jeffrey?" the medicine man inquired heartily.

"Dollar?" Halsyon whined. "Kin baby have a dollar?"

"I've brought an old friend, Jeffrey. You remember
Mr. Derelict?"

"Dollar," Halsyon whined. "Baby wants a dollar."

"What happened to the last one, Jeffrey? You haven't
finished it yet, have you?"

Halsyon sat on the bill to conceal it, but the medicine
man was too quick for him. He snatched it up and he
and the stranger-man examined it.

"As great as all the rest," Derelict sighed. "Greater!
What a magnificent talent wasting away. . . ."

Halsyon began to weep. "Baby wants a dollar!" he
cried.

The stranger man took out his wallet, selected a dollar bill and handed it to Halsyon. As soon as Halsyon touched it, he heard it sing and he tried to sing with it, but it was singing him a private song so he had to listen.

It was a lovely dollar; smooth but not too new, with a faintly matte surface that would take ink like kisses. George Washington looked reproachful but resigned, as though he was used to the treatment in store for him. And indeed he might well be, for he was much older on this dollar. Much older than on any other for his serial number was 5,271,009 which made him 5,000,-000 years old and more, and the oldest he had ever been before was 2,000,000.

As Halsyon squatted contentedly on the floor and dipped his pen in the ink as the dollar told him to, he heard the medicine man say, "I don't think I should leave you alone with him, Mr. Derelict."

"No, we must be alone together, doctor. Jeff always was shy about his work. He could only discuss it with me privately."

"How much time would you need?"

"Give me an hour."

"I doubt very much whether it'll do any good."

"But there's no harm trying?"

"I suppose not. All right, Mr. Derelict. Call the nurse when you're through."

The door opened; the door closed. The stranger-man named Derelict put his hand on Halsyon's shoulder in a friendly, intimate way. Halsyon looked up at him and grinned cleverly, meanwhile waiting for the sound of the bolt in the door. It came; like a shot, like a final nail in a coffin.

"Jeff, I've brought some of your old work with me," Derelict said in a voice that was only approximately casual. "I thought you might like to look it over with me."

"Have you got a watch on you?" Halsyon asked.

Restraining his start of surprise at Halsyon's normal tone, the art dealer took out his pocket watch and displayed it.

"Lend it to me for a minute."

Derelict unchained the watch and handed it over. Halsyon took it carefully and said, "All right. Go ahead with the pictures."

"Jeff!" Derelict exclaimed. "This is you again, isn't it? This is the way you always—"

"Thirty," Halsyon interrupted. "Thirty-five, forty, forty-five, fifty, fifty-five, ONE." He concentrated on the flicking second hand with rapt expectation.

"No, I guess it isn't," the dealer muttered. "I only imagined you sounded—Oh well." He opened the portfolio and began sorting mounted drawings.

"Forty, forty-five, fifty, fifty-five, TWO."

"Here's one of your earliest, Jeff. Remember when you came into the gallery with the roughs and we thought you were the new polisher from the agency? Took you months to forgive us. You always claimed we bought your first picture just to apologize. Do you still think so?"

"Forty, forty-five, fifty, fifty-five, THREE."

"Here's that tempera that gave you so many heartaches. I was wondering if you'd care to try another? I really don't think tempera is as inflexible as you claim and I'd be interested to have you try again now that your technique's so much more matured. What do you say?"

"Forty, forty-five, fifty, fifty-five, FOUR."

"Jeff, put down that watch."

"Ten, fifteen, twenty, twenty-five . . ."

"What the devil's the point of counting minutes?"

"Well," Halsyon said reasonably, "sometimes they lock the door and go away. Other times they lock up and stay and spy on you. But they never spy longer than three minutes so I'm giving them five just to make sure. FIVE."

Halsyon gripped the pocket watch in his big fist and drove the fist cleanly into Derelict's jaw. The dealer dropped without a sound. Halsyon dragged him to the wall, stripped him naked, dressed himself in his clothes, repacked the portfolio and closed it. He picked up the dollar bill and pocketed it. He picked up the bottle of carbon ink warranted nonpoisonous and smeared the contents over his face.

Choking and shouting, he brought the nurse to the door.

"Let me out of here," Halsyon cried in a muffled voice. "That maniac tried to drown me. Threw ink in my face. I want out!"

The door was unbolted and opened. Halsyon shoved past the nurse-man, cunningly mopping his blackened face with a hand that only masked it more. As the nurse-man started to enter the cell, Halsyon said, "Never mind

Halsyon. He's all right. Get me a towel or something. Hurry!"

The nurse-man locked the door again, turned and ran down the corridor. Halsyon waited until he disappeared into a supply room, then turned and ran in the opposite direction. He went through the heavy doors to the main wing corridor, still cleverly mopping, still sputtering with cunning indignation. He reached the main building. He was halfway out and still no alarm. He knew those brazen bells. They tested them every Wednesday noon.

It's like a game, he told himself. It's fun. It's nothing to be scared of. It's being safely, sanely, joyously a kid again and when we quit playing, I'm going home to mama and dinner and papa reading me the funnies and I'm a kid again, really a kid again, forever.

There still was no hue and cry when he reached the main floor. He complained about his indignity to the receptionist. He complained to the protection guards as he forged James Derelict's name in the visitors' book, and his inky hand smeared such a mess on the page that the forgery was undetected. The guard buzzed the final gate open. Halsyon passed through into the street, and as he started away he heard the brass of the bells begin a clattering that terrified him.

He ran. He stopped. He tried to stroll. He could not. He lurched down the street until he heard the guards shouting. He darted around a corner, and another, tore up endless streets, heard cars behind him, sirens, bells, shouts, commands. It was a ghastly Catherine Wheel of flight. Searching desperately for a hiding place, Halsyon darted into the hallway of a desolate tenement.

Halsyon began to climb the stairs. He went up three at a clip, then two, then struggled step by step as his strength failed and panic paralyzed him. He stumbled at a landing and fell against a door. The door opened. The Faraway Fiend stood within, smiling briskly, rubbing his hands.

"Glückliche Reise," he said. "On the dot. God damn. You twenty-three skidooed, eh? Enter, my old. I'm expecting you. Be it never so humble . . ."

Halsyon screamed.

"No, no, no! No Sturm und Drang, my beauty," Mr. Aquila clapped a hand over Halsyon's mouth, heaved him up, dragged him through the doorway and slammed the door.

"Presto-changeo," he laughed. "Exit Jeffrey Halsyon from mortal ken. Dieu vous garde."

Halsyon freed his mouth, screamed again and fought hysterically, biting and kicking. Mr. Aquila made a clucking noise, dipped into his pocket and brought out a package of cigarettes. He flipped one out of the pack expertly and broke it under Halsyon's nose. The artist at once subsided and suffered himself to be led to a couch, where Aquila cleansed the ink from his face and hands.

"Better, eh?" Mr. Aquila chuckled. "Non habit-forming. God damn. Drinks now called for."

He filled a shot glass from a decanter, added a tiny cube of purple ice from a fuming bucket, and placed the drink in Halsyon's hand. Compelled by a gesture from Aquila, the artist drank it off. It made his brain buzz. He stared around, breathing heavily. He was in what appeared to be the luxurious waiting room of a Park Avenue physician. Queen Anne furniture. Axminster rug. Two Hogarths and a Copley on the wall in gilt frames. They were genuine, Halsyon realized with amazement. Then, with even more amazement, he realized that he was thinking with coherence, with continuity. His mind was quite clear.

He passed a heavy hand over his forehead. "What's happened?" he asked faintly. "There's like . . . Something like a fever behind me. Nightmares."

"You have been sick," Aquila replied. "I am blunt, my old. This is a temporary return to sanity. It is no feat, God damn. Any doctor can do it. Niacin plus carbon dioxide. Id genus omne. Only temporary. We must search for something more permanent."

"What's this place?"

"Here? My office. Anteroom without. Consultation room within. Laboratory to left. In God we trust."

"I know you," Halsyon mumbled. "I know you from somewhere. I know your face."

"Oui. You have drawn and redrawn me in your fever. Ecce homo. But you have the advantage, Halsyon. Where have we met? I ask myself." Aquila put on a brilliant speculum, tilted it over his left eye and let it shine into Halsyon's face. "Now I ask you. Where have we met?"

Hypnotized by the light, Halsyon answered dreamily. "At the Beaux Arts Ball . . . A long time ago. . . . Before the fever . . ."

"Ah? Si. It was one half year ago. I was there. An unfortunate night."

"No. A glorious night . . . Gay, happy fun . . . Like a school dance . . . Like a prom in costume . . ."

"Always back to the childhood, eh?" Mr. Aquila murmured. "We must attend to that. Cetera desunt, young Lochinvar. Continue."

"I was with Judy. . . . We realized we were in love that night. We realized how wonderful life was going to be. And then you passed and looked at me. . . . Just once. You looked at me. It was horrible."

"Tch!" Mr. Aquila clicked his tongue in vexation. "Now I remember said incident. I was unguarded. Bad news from home. A pox on both my houses."

"You passed in red and black. . . . Satanic. Wearing no mask. You looked at me . . . A red and black look I never forgot. A look from black eyes like pools of hell, like cold fires of terror. And with that look you robbed me of everything . . . of joy, of hope, of love, of life. . . ."

"No, no!" Mr. Aquila said sharply. "Let us understand ourselves. My carelessness was the key that unlocked the door. But you fell into a chasm of your own making. Nevertheless, old beer and skittles, we must alter same." He removed the speculum and shook his finger at Halsyon. "We must bring you back to the land of the living. Auxilium ab alto. Jeez. That is for why I have arranged this meeting. What I have done I will undone, eh? But you you must climb out of your own chasm. Knit up the ravelled sleave of care. Come inside."

He took Halsyon's arm, led him down a paneled hall, past a neat office and into a spanking white laboratory. It was all tile and glass with shelves of reagent bottles, porcelain filters, an electric oven, stock jars of acids, bins of raw materials. There was a small round elevation in the center of the floor, a sort of dais. Mr. Aquila placed a stool on the dais, placed Halsyon on the stool, got into a white lab coat and began to assemble apparatus.

"You," he chatted, "are an artist of the utmost. I do not dorer la pilule. When Jimmy Derelict told me you were no longer at work, God damn! We must return him to his muttons, I said. Solon Aquila must own many canvases of Jeffrey Halsyon. We shall cure him. Hoc age."

"You're a doctor?" Halsyon asked.

"No. Let us say, a warlock. Strictly speaking a witch-pathologist. Very high class. No nostrums. Strictly modern magic. Black magic and white magic are passé, n'est-ce pas? I cover entire spectrum, specializing mostly in the 15,000 angstrom band."

"You're a witch-doctor? Never!"

"Oh yes."

"In this kind of place?"

"Ah-ha? You too are deceived, eh? It is our camouflage. Many a modern laboratory you think concerns itself with tooth paste is devoted to magic. But we are scientific too. Parbleu! We move with the times, we warlocks. Witch's Brew now complies with Pure Food and Drug Act. Familiars 100 per cent sterile. Sanitary brooms. Cellophane-wrapped curses. Father Satan in rubber gloves. Thanks to Lord Lister; or is it Pasteur? My idol."

The witch-pathologist gathered raw materials, consulted an ephemeris, ran off some calculations on an electronic computer and continued to chat.

"Fugit hora," Aquila said. "Your trouble, my old, is loss of sanity. Oui? Lost in one damn flight from reality and one damn desperate search for peace brought on by one unguarded look from me to you. Hélas! I apologize for that, R.S.V.P." With what looked like a miniature tennis line-marker, he rolled a circle around Halsyon on the dais. "But your trouble is, to wit: You search for the peace of infancy. You should be fighting to acquire the peace of maturity, n'est-ce pas? Jeez."

Aquila drew circles and pentagons with a glittering compass and rule, weighed out powders on a microbeam balance, dropped various liquids into crucibles from calibrated burettes, and continued: "Many warlocks do brisk trade in potions from Fountains of Youths. Oh yes. Are many youths and many fountains; but none for you. No. Youth is not for artists. Age is the cure. We must purge your youth and grow you up, nicht wahr?"

"No," Halsyon argued. "No. Youth is the art. Youth is the dream. Youth is the blessing."

"For some, yes. For many, not. Not for you. You are cursed, my adolescent. We must purge you. Lust for power. Lust for sex. Injustice collecting. Escape from reality. Passion for revenges. Oh yes, Father Freud is also my idol. We wipe your slate clean at very small price."

"What price?"

"You will see when we are finished."

Mr. Aquila deposited liquids and powders around the

helpless artist in crucibles and petri dishes. He measured and cut fuses, set up a train from the circle to an electric timer which he carefully adjusted. He went to a shelf of serum bottles, took down a small Woulff vial numbered 5-271-009, filled a syringe and meticulously injected Halsyon.

"We begin," he said, "the purge of your dreams. Voilá."

He tripped the electric timer and stepped behind a lead shield. There was a moment of silence. Suddenly black music crashed from a concealed loudspeaker and a recorded voice began an intolerable chant. In quick succession the powders and liquids around Halsyon burst into flame. He was engulfed in music and fire. The world began to spin around him in a roaring confusion. . . .

The president of the United Nations came to him. He was tall and gaunt, sprightly but bitter. He was wringing his hands in dismay.

"Mr. Halsyon! Mr. Halsyon!" he cried. "Where you been, my cupcake? God damn. Hoc tempore. Do you know what has happened?"

"No," Halsyon answered. "What's happened?"

"After your escape from the looney bin. Bango! Atom bombs everywhere. The two-hour war. It is over. Hora fugit, old faithful, Virility is over."

"What!"

"Hard radiation, Mr. Halsyon, has destroyed the virility of the world. God damn. You are the only man left capable of engendering children. No doubt on account of a mysterious mutant strain in your makeup which it makes you different. Jeez."

"No."

"Oui. It is your responsibility to repopulate the world. We have taken for you a suite at the Odeon. It has three bedrooms. Three; my favorite. A prime number."

"Hot dog!" Halsyon said. "This is my big dream."

His progress to the Odeon was a triumph. He was garlanded with flowers, serenaded, hailed and cheered. Ecstatic women displayed themselves wickedly before him, begging for his attention. In his suite, Halsyon was wined and dined. A tall, gaunt man entered subserviently. He was sprightly but bitter. He had a list in his hand.

"I am World Procurer at your service, Mr. Halsyon,"

he said. He consulted his list. "God damn. Are 5,271,009 virgins clamoring for your attention. All guaranteed beautiful. Ewig-Weibliche. Pick a number from one to 5,000,-000."

"We'll start with a redhead," Halsyon said.

They brought him a redhead. She was slender and boyish, with a small hard bosom. The next was fuller with a rollicking rump. The fifth was Junoesque and her breasts were like African pears. The tenth was a voluptuous Rembrandt. The twentieth was wiry. The thirtieth was slender and boyish with a small hard bosom.

"Haven't we met before?" Halsyon inquired.

"No," she said.

The next was fuller with a rollicking rump.

"The body is familiar," Halsyon said.

"No," she answered.

The fiftieth was Junoesque with breasts like African pears.

"Surely?" Halsyon said.

"Never," she answered.

The World Procurer entered with Halsyon's morning aphrodisiac.

"Never touch the stuff," Halsyon said.

"God damn," the Procurer exclaimed. "You are a veritable giant. An elephant. No wonder you are the beloved Adam. Tant soit peu. No wonder they all weep for love of you." He drank off the aphrodisiac himself.

"Have you noticed they're all getting to look alike?" Halsyon complained.

"But no! Are all different. Parbleu! This is an insult to my office."

"Oh, they're different from one to another, but the types keep repeating."

"Ah? This is life, my old. All life is cyclic. Have you not, as an artist, noticed?"

"I didn't think it applied to love."

"To all things. Wahrheit und Dichtung."

"What was that you said about them weeping?"

"Oui. They all weep."

"Why?"

"For ecstatic love of you. God damn."

Halsyon thought over the succession of boyish, rollicking, Junoesque, Rembrandtesque, wiry, red, blonde, brunette, white, black and brown women.

"I hadn't noticed," he said.

"Observe today, my world father. Shall we commence?"

It was true. Halsyon hadn't noticed. They all wept. He was flattered but depressed.

"Why don't you laugh a little?" he asked.

They would not or could not.

Upstairs on the Odeon roof where Halsyon took his afternoon exercise, he questioned his trainer who was a tall, gaunt man with a sprightly but bitter expression.

"Ah?" said the trainer. "God damn. I don't know, old Scotch and soda. Perhaps because it is a traumatic experience for them."

"Traumatic?" Halsyon puffed. "Why? What do I do to them?"

"Ah-ha? You joke, eh? All the world knows what you do to them."

"No, I mean . . . How can it be traumatic? They're all fighting to get to me, aren't they? Don't I come up to expectations?"

"A mystery. Tripotage. Now, beloved father of the world, we practice the push-ups. Ready? Begin."

Downstairs, in the Odeon restaurant, Halsyon questioned the headwaiter, a tall, gaunt man with a sprightly manner but bitter expression.

"We are men of the world, Mr. Halsyon. Suo jure. Surely you understand. These women love you and can expect no more than one night of love. God damn. Naturally they are disappointed."

"What do they want?"

"What every woman wants, my gateway to the west. A permanent relationship. Marriage."

"Marriage!"

"Oui."

"All of them?"

"Oui."

"All right. I'll marry all 5,271,009."

But the World Procurer objected. "No, no, no, young Lochinvar. God damn. Impossible. Aside from religious difficulties there are human also. Who could manage such a harem?"

"Then I'll marry one."

"No, no, no. Pensez à moi. How could you make the choice? How could you select? By lottery, drawing straws, tossing coins?"

"I've already selected one."

"Ah? Which?"

"My girl," Halsyon said slowly. "Judith Field."

"So. Your sweetheart?"

"Yes."

"She is far down on the list of 5,000,000."

"She's always been number one on my list. I want Judith." Halsyon sighed. "I remember how she looked at the Beaux Arts Ball. . . . There was a full moon. . . ."

"But there will be no full moon until the twenty-sixth."

"I want Judith."

"The others will tear her apart out of jealousy. No, no, no, Mr. Halsyon, we must stick to the schedule. One night for all, no more for any."

"I want Judith . . . or else."

"It will have to be discussed in council. God damn."

It was discussed in the U. N. council by a dozen delegates, all tall, gaunt, sprightly but bitter. It was decided to permit Jeffrey Halsyon one secret marriage.

"But no domestic ties," the World Procurer warned. "No faithfulness to your wife. That must be understood. We cannot spare you from our program. You are indispensable."

They brought the lucky Judith Field to the Odeon. She was a tall, dark girl with cropped curly hair and lovely tennis legs. Halsyon took her hand. The World Procurer tip-toed out.

"Hello, darling," Halsyon murmured.

Judith looked at him with loathing. Her eyes were wet, her face was bruised from weeping.

"Hello, darling," Halsyon repeated.

"If you touch me, Jeff," Judith said in a strangled voice, "I'll kill you."

"Judy!"

"That disgusting man explained everything to me. He didn't seem to understand when I tried to explain to him. . . . I was praying you'd be dead before it was my turn."

"But this is marriage, Judy."

"I'd rather die than be married to you."

"I don't believe you. We've been in love for—"

"For God's sake, Jeff, love's over for you. Don't you understand? Those women cry because they hate you. I hate you. The world loathes you. You're disgusting."

Halsyon stared at the girl and saw the truth in her face. In an excess of rage he tried to seize her. She fought him bitterly. They careened around the huge living room of the suite, overturning furniture, their breath hissing, their fury mounting. Halsyon struck Judith Field with his big fist to end the struggle once and for all. She reeled back, clutched at a drape, smashed through a french window and fell fourteen floors to the street like a gyrating doll.

Halsyon looked down in horror. A crowd gathered around the smashed body. Faces upturned. Fists shook. An ominous growl began. The World Procurer dashed into the suite.

"My old! My blue!" he cried. "What have you done? Per conto. It is a spark that will ignite savagery. You are in very grave danger. God damn."

"Is it true they all hate me?"

"Hélas, then you have discovered the truth? That indiscreet girl. I warned her. Oui. You are loathed."

"But you told me I was loved. The new Adam. Father of the new world."

"Oui. You are the father, but what child does not hate its father? You are also a legal rapist. What woman does not hate being forced to embrace a man . . . even by necessity for survival? Come quickly, my rock and rye. Passim. You are in great danger."

He dragged Halsyon to a back elevator and took him down to the Odeon cellar.

"The army will get you out. We take you to Turkey at once and effect a compromise."

Halsyon was transferred to the custody of a tall, gaunt, bitter army colonel who rushed him through underground passages to a side street, where a staff car was waiting. The colonel thrust Halsyon inside.

"Jacta alea est," he said to the driver. "Speed, my corporal. Protect old faithful. To the airport. Alors!"

"God damn, sir," the corporal replied. He saluted and started the car. As it twisted through the streets at break-neck speed, Halsyon glanced at him. He was a tall, gaunt man, sprightly but bitter.

"Kulturkampf der Menscheit," the corporal muttered. "Jeez!"

A giant barricade had been built across the street, improvised of ash barrels, furniture, overturned cars, traffic stanchions. The corporal was forced to brake the car. As he slowed for a U-turn, a mob of women appeared from doorways, cellars, stores. They were screaming. Some of them brandished improvised clubs.

"Excelsior!" the corporal cried. "God damn." He tried

to pull his service gun out of its holster. The women yanked open the car doors and tore Halsyon and the corporal out. Halsyon broke free, struggled through the wild clubbing mob, dashed to the sidewalk, stumbled and dropped with a sickening yaw through an open coal chute. He shot down and spilled out into an endless black space. His head whirled. A stream of stars sailed before his eyes. . . .

And he drifted alone in space, a martyr, misunderstood, a victim of cruel injustice.

He was still chained to what had once been the wall of Cell 5, Block 27, Tier 100, Wing 9 of the Callisto Penitentiary until that unexpected gamma explosion had torn the vast fortress dungeon—Vaster than the Chateau d' If—apart. That explosion, he realized, had been detonated by the Grssh.

His assets were his convict clothes, a helmet, one cylinder of O_2, his grim fury at the injustice that had been done him, and his knowledge of the secret of how the Grssh could be defeated in their maniacal quest for solar domination.

The Grssh, ghastly marauders from Omicron Ceti, space-degenerates, space-imperialists, cold-blooded, roachlike, depending for their food upon the psychotic horrors which they engendered in man through mental control and upon which they fed, were rapidly conquering the galaxy. There were irrestible, for they possessed the power of simul-kinesis—the ability to be in two places at the same time.

Against the vault of space, a dot of light moved, slowly, like a stricken meteor. It was a rescue ship, Halsyon realized, combing space for survivors of the explosion. He wondered whether the light of Jupiter, flooding him with rusty radiation, would make him visible to the rescuers. He wondered whether he wanted to be rescued at all.

"It will be the same thing again," Halsyon grated. "Falsely accused by Balorsen's robot. . . . Falsely convicted by Judith's father. . . . Repudiated by Judith herself. . . . Jailed again . . . and finally destroyed by the Grssh as they destroy the last strongholds of Terra. Why not die now?"

But even as he spoke he realized he lied. He was the one man with the one secret that could save the earth and the very galaxy itself. He must survive. He must fight.

With indomitable will, Halsyon struggled to his feet, fighting the constricting chains. With the steely strength he had developed as a penal laborer in the Grssh mines, he waved and shouted. The spot of light did not alter its slow course away from him. Then he saw the metal link of one of his chains strike a brilliant spark from the flinty rock. He resolved on a desperate expedient to signal the rescue ship.

He detached the plasti-hose of the O_2 tank from his plasti-helmet, and permitted the stream of life-giving oxygen to spurt into space. With trembling hands, he gathered the links of his leg chain and dashed them against the rock under the oxygen. A spark glowed. The oxygen caught fire. A brilliant geyser of white flame spurted for half a mile into space.

Husbanding the last oxygen in his plasti-helmet, Halsyon twisted the cylinder slowly, sweeping the fan of flame back and forth in a last desperate bid for rescue. The atmosphere in his plasti-helmet grew foul and acrid. His ears roared. His sight flickered. At last his senses failed. . . .

When he recovered consciousness he was in a plasti-cot in the cabin of a starship. The high frequency whine told him they were in overdrive. He opened his eyes. Balorsen stood before the plasti-cot, and Balorsen's robot and High Judge Field, and his daughter Judith. Judith was weeping. The robot was in magnetic plasti-clamps and winced as General Balorsen lashed him again and again with a nuclear, plasti-whip.

"Parbleu! God damn!" the robot grated. "It is true I framed Jeff Halsyon. Ouch! Flux de bouche. I was the space-pirate who space-hijacked the space-freighter. God damn. Ouch! The space-bartender in the Spaceman's Saloon was my accomplice. When Jackson wrecked the space-cab I went to the space-garage and X-beamed the sonic *before* Tantial murdered O'Leary. Aux armes. Jeez. Ouch!"

"There you have the confession, Halsyon," General Balorsen grated. He was tall, gaunt, bitter. "By God. Ars est celare artem. You are innocent."

"I falsely condemned you, old faithful," Judge Field grated. He was tall, gaunt, bitter. "Can you forgive this God damn fool? We apologize."

"We wronged you, Jeff," Judith whispered. "How can you ever forgive us? Say you forgive us."

"You're sorry for the way you treated me," Halsyon grated. "But it's only because on account of a mysterious mutant strain in my makeup which it makes me different, I'm the one man with the one secret that can save the galaxy from the Grssh."

"No, no, no, old gin and tonic," General Balorsen pleaded. "God damn. Don't hold grudges. Save us from the Grssh."

"Save us, faute de mieux, save us, Jeff," Judge Field put in.

"Oh please, Jeff, please," Judith whispered. "The Grssh are everywhere and coming closer. We're taking you to the U. N. You must tell the council how to stop the Grssh from being in two places at the same time."

The starship came out of overdrive and landed on Governor's Island where a delegation of world dignitaries met the ship and rushed Halsyon to the General Assembly room of the U. N. They drove down the strangely rounded streets lined with strangely rounded buildings which had all been altered when it was discovered that the Grssh always appeared in corners. There was not a corner or an angle left on all Terra.

The General Assembly was filled when Halsyon entered. Hundreds of tall, gaunt, bitter diplomats applauded as he made his way to the podium, still dressed in convict plasti-clothes. Halsyon looked around resentfully.

"Yes," he grated. "You all applaud. You all revere me now; but where were you when I was framed, convicted and jailed . . . an innocent man? Where were you then?"

"Halsyon, forgive us. God damn!" they shouted.

"I will not forgive you, I suffered for seventeen years in the Grssh mines. Now it's your turn to suffer."

"Please, Halsyon!"

"Where are your experts? Your professors? Your specialists? Where are your electronic calculators? Your super thinking machines? Let them solve the mystery of the Grssh."

"They can't, old whiskey and soda. Entre nous. They're stopped cold. Save us, Halsyon. Auf wiedersehen."

Judith took his arm. "Not for my sake, Jeff," she whispered. "I know you'll never forgive me for the injustice I did you. But for the sake of all the other girls in the galaxy who love and are loved."

"I still love you, Judy."

"I've always loved you, Jeff."

"Okay. I didn't want to tell them but you talked me

into it." Halsyon raised his hand for silence. In the ensuing hush he spoke softly. "The secret is this, gentlemen. Your calculators have assembled data to ferret out the secret weakness of the Grssh. They have not been able to find any. Consequently you have assumed that the Grssh have no secret weakness. *That was a wrong assumption."*

The General Assembly held its breath.

"Here is the secret. *You should have assumed there was something wrong with the calculators."*

"God damn!" the General Assembly cried. "Why didn't we think of that? God damn!"

"And I know what's wrong!"

There was a deathlike hush.

The door of the General Assembly burst open. Professor Deathhush, tall, gaunt, bitter, tottered in. "Eureka!" he cried. "I've found it. God damn. Something wrong with the thinking machines. Three comes *after* two, not before."

The General Assembly broke into cheers. Professor Deathhush was seized and pummeled happily. Bottles were opened. His health was drunk. Several medals were pinned on him. He beamed.

"Hey!" Halsyon called. "That was my secret. I'm the one man who on account of a mysterious mutant strain in my—"

The ticker-tape began pounding: ATTENTION. ATTENTION. HUSHENKOV IN MOSCOW REPORTS DEFECT IN CALCULATORS. 3 COMES AFTER 2 AND NOT BEFORE, REPEAT: AFTER (UNDERSCORE) NOT BEFORE.

A postman ran in. "Special delivery from Doctor Lifehush at Caltech. Says something's wrong with the thinking machines. Three comes after two, not before."

A telegraph boy delivered a wire: THINKING MACHINE WRONG STOP TWO COMES BEFORE THREE STOP NOT AFTER STOP. VON DREAMHUSH, HEIDELBERG.

A bottle was thrown through the window. It crashed on the floor revealing a bit of paper on which was scrawled: *Did you ever stopp to thinc that maibe the number 3 comes after 2 insted of in front? Down with the Grish. Mr. Hush-Hush.*

Halsyon buttonholed Judge Field. "What the hell is this?" he demanded. "I thought I was the one man in the world with that secret."

"HimmelHerrGott!" Judge Field replied impatiently. "You are all alike. You dream you are the one men with a secret, the one men with a wrong, the one men with an injustice, with a girl, without a girl, with or without anything. God damn. You bore me, you one-man dreamers. Get lost."

Judge Field shouldered him aside. General Balorsen shoved him back. Judith Field ignored him. Balorsen's robot sneakily tripped him into a corner of the crowd where a Grssh, also in a crowded corner on Neptune, appeared, did something unspeakable to Halsyon and disappeared with him, screaming, jerking and sobbing into a horror that was a delicious meal for the Grssh but a plasti-nightmare for Halsyon . . .

From which his mother awakened him and said, "This'll teach you not to sneak peanut-butter sandwiches in the middle of the night. Jeffrey."

"Mama?"

"Yes. It's time to get up, dear. You'll be late for school."

She left the room. He looked around. He looked at himself. It was true. True! The glorious realization came upon him. His dream had come true. He was ten years old again, in the flesh that was his ten-year-old body, in the home that was his boyhood home, in the life that had been his life in the nineteen thirties. And within his head was the knowledge, the experience, the sophistication of a man of thirty-three.

"Oh joy!" he cried. "It'll be a triumph. A triumph!"

He would be the school genius. He would astonish his parents, amaze his teachers, confound the experts. He would win scholarships. He would settle the hash of that kid Rennahan who used to bully him. He would hire a typewriter and write all the successful plays and stories and novels he remembered. He would cash in on that lost opportunity with Judy Field behind the memorial in Isham Park. He would steal inventions and discoveries, get in on the ground floor of new industries, make bets, play the stockmarket. He would own the world by the time he caught up with himself.

He dressed with difficulty. He had forgotten where his clothes were kept. He ate breakfast with difficulty. This was no time to explain to his mother that he'd gotten into the habit of starting the day with Irish coffee. He missed his morning cigarette. He had no idea where his school-books were. His mother had trouble starting him out.

"Jeff's in one of his moods," he heard her mutter. "I hope he gets through the day."

The day started with Rennahan ambushing him at the Boy's Entrance. Halsyon remembered him as a big tough kid with a vicious expression. He was astonished to discover that Rennahan was skinny and harassed, and obviously compelled by some bedevilments to be omnivorously aggressive.

"Why, you're not hostile to me," Halsyon exclaimed. "You're just a mixed-up kid who's trying to prove something."

Rennahan punched him.

"Look, kid," Halsyon said kindly. "You really want to be friends with the world. You're just insecure. That's why you're compelled to fight."

Rennahan was deaf to spot analysis. He punched Halsyon harder. It hurt.

"Oh leave me alone," Halsyon said. "Go prove yourself on somebody else."

Rennahan, with two swift motions, knocked Halsyon's books from under his arm and ripped his fly open. There was nothing for it but to fight. Twenty years of watching films of the future Joe Louis did nothing for Halsyon. He was thoroughly licked. He was also late for school. Now was his chance to amaze his teachers.

"The fact is," he explained to Miss Ralph of the fifth grade. "I had a run-in with a neurotic. I can speak for his left hook but I won't answer for his compulsions."

Miss Ralph slapped him and sent him to the principal with a note, reporting unheard-of insolence.

"The only thing unheard of in this school," Halsyon told Mr. Snider, "is psychoanalysis. How can you pretend to be competent teachers if you don't—"

"Dirty little boy!" Mr. Snider interrupted angrily. He was tall, gaunt, bitter. "So you've been reading dirty books, eh?"

"What the hell's dirty about Freud?"

"And using profane language, eh? You need a lesson, you filthy little animal."

He was sent home with a note requesting an immediate consultation with his parents regarding the withdrawal of Jeffrey Halsyon from school as a degenerate in desperate need of correction and vocational guidance.

Instead of going home he went to a newsstand to check the papers for events on which to get a bet down. The headlines were full of the pennant race. But who the hell won the pennant in 1931? And the series? He couldn't for the life of him remember. And the stock market? He couldn't remember anything about that either. He'd never been particularly interested in such matters as a boy. There was nothing planted in his memory to call upon.

He tried to get into the library for further checks. The librarian, tall, gaunt, and bitter, would not permit him to enter until children's hour in the afternoon. He loafed on the streets. Wherever he loafed he was chased by gaunt and bitter adults. He was beginning to realize that ten-year-old boys had limited opportunities to amaze the world.

At lunch hour he met Judy Field and accompanied her home from school. He was appalled by her knobby knees and black corkscrew curls. He didn't like the way she smelled either. But he was rather taken with her mother who was the image of the Judy he remembered. He forgot himself with Mrs. Field and did one or two things that indeed confounded her. She drove him out of the house and then telephoned his mother, her voice shaking with indignation.

Halsyon went down to the Hudson River and hung around the ferry docks until he was chased. He went to a stationery store to inquire about typewriter rentals and was chased. He searched for a quiet place to sit, think, plan, perhaps begin the recall of a successful story. There was no quiet place to which a small boy would be admitted.

He slipped into his house at 4:30, dropped his books in his room, stole into the living room, sneaked a cigarette and was on his way out when he discovered his mother and father inspecting him. His mother looked shocked. His father was gaunt and bitter.

"Oh," Halsyon said. "I suppose Snider phoned. I'd forgotten about that."

"*Mister* Snider," his mother said.

"And Mrs. Field," his father said.

"Look," Halsyon began. "We'd better get this straightened out. Will you listen to me for a few minutes? I have something startling to tell you and we've got to plan what to do about it. I—"

He yelped. His father had taken him by the ear and

was marching him down the hall. Parents did not listen
to children for a few minutes. They did not listen at all.

"Pop . . . Just a minute . . . Please! I'm trying to explain. I'm not really ten years old. I'm thirty-three.
There's been a freak in time, see? On account of a mysterious mutant strain in my makeup which—"

"Damn you! Be quiet!" his father shouted. The pain of
his big hands, the suppressed fury in his voice silenced
Halsyon. He suffered himself to be led out of the house,
down four blocks to the school, and up one flight to Mr.
Snider's office where a public school psychologist was
waiting with the principal. He was a tall man, gaunt, bitter, but sprightly.

"Ah yes, yes," he said. "So this is our little degenerate.
Our Scarface Al Capone, eh? Come, we take him to the
clinic and there I shall take his journal intime. We will
hope for the best. Nisi prius. He cannot be all bad."

He took Halsyon's arm. Halsyon pulled his arm away
and said, "Listen, you're an adult, intelligent man. You'll
listen to me. My father's got emotional problems that
blind him to the—"

His father gave him a tremendous box on the ear,
grabbed his arm and thrust it back into the psychologist's
grasp. Halsyon burst into tears. The psychologist led him
out of the office and into the tiny school infirmary. Halsyon was hysterical. He was trembling with frustration
and terror.

"Won't anybody listen to me?" he sobbed. "Won't anybody try to understand? Is this what we're all like to
kids? Is this what all kids go through?"

"Gently, my sausage," the psychologist murmured. He
popped a pill into Halsyon's mouth and forced him to
drink some water.

"You're all so damned inhuman," Halsyon wept. "You
keep us out of your world, but you keep barging into ours.
If you don't respect us why don't you leave us alone?"

"You begin to understand, eh?" the psychologist said.
"We are two different breeds of animal, childrens and
adults. God damn. I speak to you with frankness. Les
absents ont toujours tort. There is no meetings of the
minds. Jeez. There is nothing but war. It is why all childrens grow up hating their childhoods and searching for
revenges. But there is never revenges. Pari mutuel. How
can there be? Can a cat insult a king?"

"It's . . . S'hateful," Halsyon mumbled. The pill was

taking effect rapidly. "Whole world's hateful. Full of conflicts'n'insults 'at can't be r'solved . . . or paid back. . . .
S'like a joke somebody's playin' on us. Silly joke without
point. Isn't?"

As he slid down into darkness, he could hear the psychologist chuckle, but couldn't for the life of him understand what he was laughing at. . . .

He picked up his spade and followed the first clown
into the cemetery. The first clown was a tall man, gaunt,
bitter, but sprightly.

"Is she to be buried in Christian burial that wilfully
seeks her own salvation?" the first clown asked.

"I tell thee she is," Halsyon answered. "And therefore
make her grave straight: the crowner hath sat on her,
and finds it Christian burial."

"How can that be, unless she drowned herself in her
own defense?"

"Why, 'tis found so."

They began to dig the grave. The first clown thought
the matter over, then said, "It must be *se offendendo;* it
cannot be else. For here lies the point: if I drown myself
wittingly, it argues an act: and an act hath three branches;
it is, to act, to do, to perform: argal, she drowned herself wittingly."

"Nay, but hear you, goodman delver—" Halsyon began.

"Give me leave," the first clown interrupted and went
on with a tiresome discourse on quest-law. Then he turned
sprightly and cracked a few professional jokes. At last
Halsyon got away and went down to Yaughan's for a
drink. When he returned, the first clown was cracking
jokes with a couple of gentlemen who had wandered into
the graveyard. One of them made quite a fuss about a
skull.

The burial procession arrived; the coffin, the dead girl's
brother, the king and queen, the priests and lords. They
buried her, and the brother and one of the gentlemen
began to quarrel over her grave. Halsyon paid no attention. There was a pretty girl in the procession, dark, with
cropped curly hair and lovely long legs. He winked at her.
She winked back. Halsyon edged over toward her, speaking with his eyes and she answered him saucily the same
way.

Then he picked up his spade and followed the first

clown into the cemetery. The first clown was a tall man, gaunt, with a bitter expression but a sprightly manner.

"Is she to be buried in Christian burial that wilfully seeks her own salvation?" the first clown asked.

"I tell thee she is," Halsyon answered. "And therefore make her grave straight: the crowner hath sat on her, and finds it Christian burial."

"How can that be, unless she drowned herself in her own defense?"

"Didn't you ask me that before?" Halsyon inquired.

"Shut up, old faithful. Answer the question."

"I could swear this happened before."

"God damn. Will you answer? Jeez."

"Why, 'tis found so."

They began to dig the grave. The first clown thought the matter over and began a long discourse on quest-law. After that he turned sprightly and cracked trade jokes. At last Halsyon got away and went down to Yaughan's for a drink. When he returned there were a couple of strangers at the grave and then the burial procession arrived.

There was a pretty girl in the procession, dark, with cropped curly hair and lovely long legs. Halsyon winked at her. She winked back. Halsyon edged over toward her, speaking with his eyes and she answering him the same way.

"What's your name?" he whispered.

"Judith," she answered.

"I have your name tattooed on me, Judith."

"You're lying, sir."

"I can prove it, Madam. I'll show you where I was tattooed."

"And where is that?"

"In Yaughan's tavern. It was done by a sailor off the Golden Hind. Will you see it with me tonight?"

Before she could answer, he picked up his spade and followed the first clown into the cemetery. The first clown was a tall man, gaunt, with a bitter expression but a sprightly manner.

"For God's sake!" Halsyon complained. "I could swear this happened before."

"Is she to be buried in Christian burial that wilfully seeks her own salvation?" the first clown asked.

"I just know we've been through all this."

"Will you answer the question!"

"Listen," Halsyon said doggedly. "Maybe I'm crazy; maybe not. But I've got a spooky feeling that all this happened before. It seems unreal. Life seems unreal."

The first clown shook his head. "HimmelHerrGott," he muttered. "It is as I feared. Lux et veritas. On account of a mysterious mutant strain in your makeup which it makes you different, you are treading on thin water. Ewigkeit! Answer the question."

"If I've answered it once, I've answered it a hundred times."

"Old ham and eggs," the first clown burst out, "you have answered it 5,271,009 times. God damn. Answer again."

"Why?"

"Because you must. Pot au feu. It is the life we must live."

"You call this life? Doing the same things over and over again? Saying the same things? Winking at girls and never getting any further?"

"No, no, no, my Donner and Blitzen. Do not question. It is a conspiracy we dare not fight. This is the life every man lives. Every man does the same things over and over. There is no escape."

"Why is there no escape?"

"I dare not say; I dare not. Vox populi. Others have questioned and disappeared. It is a conspiracy. I'm afraid."

"Afraid of what?"

"Of our owners."

"What? We are owned?"

"Si. Ach, ja! All of us, young mutant. There is no reality. There is no life, no freedom, no will. God damn. Don't you realize? We are . . . We are all characters in a book. As the book is read, we dance our dances; when the book is read again, we dance again. E pluribus unum. Is she to be buried in Christian burial that wilfully seeks her own salvation?"

"What are you saying?" Halsyon cried in horror. "We're puppets?"

"Answer the question."

"If there's no freedom, no free will, how can we be talking like this?"

"Whoever's reading our book is day-dreaming, my capital of Dakota. Idem est. Answer the question."

"I will not. I'm going to revolt. I'll dance for our owners no longer. I'll find a better life. . . . I'll find reality."

"No, no! It's madness, Jeffrey! Cul-de-sac!"

"All we need is one brave leader. The rest will follow. We'll smash the conspiracy that chains us!"

"It cannot be done. Play it safe. Answer the question."

Halsyon answered the question by picking up his spade and bashing in the head of the first clown who appeared not to notice. "Is she to be buried in Christian burial that wilfully seeks her own salvation?" he asked.

"Revolt!" Halsyon cried and bashed him again. The clown started to sing. The two gentlemen appeared. One said: "Has this fellow no feeling of business that he sings at grave-making?"

"Revolt! Follow me!" Halsyon shouted and swung his spade against the gentlemen's melancholy head. He paid no attention. He chatted with his friend and the first clown. Halsyon whirled like a dervish, laying about him with his spade. The gentleman picked up a skull and philosophized over some person or persons named Yorick.

The funeral procession approached. Halsyon attacked it, whirling and turning, around and around with the clotted frenzy of a man in a dream.

"Stop reading the book," he shouted. "Let me out of the pages. Can you hear me? Stop reading the book! I'd rather be in a world of my own making. Let me go!"

There was a mighty clap of thunder, as of the covers of a mighty book slamming shut. In an instant Halsyon was swept spinning into the third compartment of the seventh circle of the Inferno in the fourteenth Canto of the Divine Comedy where they who have sinned against art are tormented by flakes of fire which are eternally showered down upon them. There he shrieked until he had provided sufficient amusement. Only then was he permitted to devise a text of his own . . . and he formed a new world, a romantic world, a world of his fondest dreams. . . .

He was the last man on earth.

He was the last man on earth and he howled.

The hills, the valleys, the mountains and streams were his, his alone, and he howled.

Five million two hundred and seventy-one thousand and nine houses were his for shelter, 5,271,009 beds were his for sleeping. The shops were his for the breaking and entering. The jewels of the world were his; the toys, the tools, the playthings, the necessities, the luxuries . . . all belonged to the last man on earth, and he howled.

He left the country mansion in the fields of Connecticut where he had taken up residence; he crossed into Westchester, howling; he ran south along what had once been the Hendrick Hudson Highway, howling; he crossed the bridge into Manhattan, howling; he ran downtown past lonely skyscrapers, department stores, amusement palaces, howling. He howled down Fifth Avenue, and at the corner of Fiftieth Street he saw a human being.

She was alive, breathing; a beautiful woman. She was tall and dark with cropped curly hair and lovely long legs. She wore a white blouse, tiger-skin riding breeches and patent leather boots. She carried a rifle. She wore a revolver on her hip. She was eating stewed tomatoes from a can and she stared at Halsyon in unbelief. He ran up to her.

"I thought I was the last human on earth," she said.

"You're the last woman," Halsyon howled. "I'm the last man. Are you a dentist?"

"No," she said. "I'm the daughter of the unfortunate Professor Field whose well-intentioned but ill-advised experiment in nuclear fission has wiped mankind off the face of the earth with the exception of you and me who, no doubt on account of some mysterious mutant strain in our makeup which it makes us different, are the last of the old civilization and the first of the new."

"Didn't your father teach you anything about dentistry?"

"No," she said.

"Then lend me your gun for a minute."

She unholstered the revolver and handed it to Halsyon, meanwhile keeping her rifle ready. Halsyon cocked the gun.

"I wish you'd been a dentist," he said.

"I'm a beautiful woman with an I.Q. of 141 which is more important for the propagation of a brave new beautiful race of men to inherit the good green earth," she said.

"Not with my teeth it isn't," Halsyon howled.

He clapped the revolver to his temple and blew his brains out.

He awoke with a splitting headache. He was lying on the tile dais alongside the stool, his bruised temple pressed against the cold floor. Mr. Aquila had emerged from the lead shield and was turning on an exhaust fan to clear the air.

"Bravo, my liver and onions," he chuckled. "The last one you did by yourself, eh? No assistance from yours truly required. Meglio tarde che mai. But you went over with a crack before I could catch you. God damn."

He helped Halsyon to his feet and led him into the consultation room where he seated him on a velvet chaise longue and gave him a glass of brandy.

"Guaranteed free of drugs," he said. "Noblesse oblige. Only the best spiritus frumenti. Now we discuss what we have done, eh? Jeez."

He sat down behind the desk, still sprightly, still bitter, and regarded Halsyon with kindliness. "Man lives by his decisions, n'est-ce pas?" he began. "We agree, oui? A man has some five million two hundred seventy-one thousand and nine decisions to make in the course of his life. Peste! It is a prime number? N'importe. Do you agree?"

Halsyon nodded.

"So, my coffee and doughnuts, it is the maturity of these decisions that decides whether a man is a man or a child. Nicht wahr? Malgré nous. A man cannot start making adult decisions until he has purged himself of the dreams of childhood. God damn. Such fantasies. They must go."

"No," Halsyon said slowly. "It's the dreams that make my art . . . the dreams and fantasies that I translate into line and color. . . ."

"God damn! Yes. Agreed. Maître d'hôtel: But adult dreams, not baby dreams. Baby dreams. Pfui! All men have them. . . . To be the last man on earth and own the earth . . . To be the last fertile man on earth and own the women . . . To go back in time with the advantage of adult knowledge and win victories . . . To escape reality with the dream that life is make-believe . . . To escape responsibility with a fantasy of heroic injustice, of martyrdom with a happy ending . . . And there are hundreds more, equally popular, equally empty. God bless Father Freud and his merry men. He applies the quietus to such nonsense. Sic semper tyrannis. Avaunt!"

"But if everybody has those dreams, they can't be bad, can they?"

"God damn. Everybody in fourteenth century had lice.

Did that make it good? No, my young, such dreams are for childrens. Too many adults are still childrens. It is you, the artists, who must lead them out as I have led you. I purge you; now you purge them."

"Why did you do this?"

"Because I have faith in you. Sic vos non vobis. It will not be easy for you. A long hard road and lonely."

"I suppose I ought to feel grateful," Halsyon muttered, "but I feel . . . well . . . empty. Cheated."

"Oh yes, God damn. If you live with one Jeez big ulcer long enough you miss him when he's cut out. You were hiding in an ulcer. I have robbed you of said refuge. Ergo: you feel cheated. Wait! You will feel even more cheated. There was a price to pay, I told you. You have paid it. Look."

Mr. Aquila held up a hand mirror. Halsyon glanced into it, then started and stared. A fifty-year-old face stared back at him: lined, hardened, solid, determined. Halsyon leaped to his feet.

"Gently, gently," Mr. Aquila admonished. "It is not so bad. It is damned good. You are still thirty-three in age of physique. You have lost none of your life . . . only all of your youth. What have you lost? A pretty face to lure young girls? Is that why you are wild?"

"Christ!" Halsyon cried.

"All right. Still gently, my child. Here you are, purged, disillusioned, unhappy, bewildered, one foot on the hard road to maturity. Would you like this to have happened or not have happened? Si. I can do. This can never have happened. Spurlos versenkt. It is ten seconds from your escape. You can have your pretty young face back. You can be recaptured. You can return to the safe ulcer of the womb . . . a child again. Would you like same?"

"You can't."

"Sauve qui peut, my Pike's Peak. I can. There is no end to the 15,000 angstrom band."

"Damn you! Are you Satan? Lucifer? Only the devil could have such powers."

"Or angels, my old."

"You don't look like an angel. You look like Satan."

"Ah? Ha? But Satan was an angel before he fell. He has many relations on high. Surely there are family resemblances. God damn." Mr. Aquila stopped laughing. He leaned across the desk and the sprightliness was gone from his face. Only the bitterness remained. "Shall I tell you who I am, my chicken? Shall I explain why one un-guarded look from this phizz toppled you over the brink?"

Halsyon nodded, unable to speak.

"I am a scoundrel, a black sheep, a scapegrace, a blackguard. I am a remittance man. Yes. God damn! I am a remittance man." Mr. Aquila's eyes turned into wounds. "By your standards I am the great man of in-finite power and variety. So was the remittance man from Europe to naive natives on the beaches of Tahiti. Eh? And so am I to you as I comb the beaches of the stars for a little amusement, a little hope, a little joy to while away the lonely years of my exile. . . .

"I am bad," Mr. Aquila said in a voice of chilling desperation. "I am rotten. There is no place in my home that can tolerate me. They pay me to stay away. And there are moments, unguarded, when my sickness and my despair fill my eyes and strike terror into your inno-cent souls. As I strike terror into you now. Yes?"

Halsyon nodded again.

"Be guided by me. It was the child in Solon Aquila that destroyed him and led him into the sickness that de-stroyed his life. Oui. I too suffer from baby fantasies from which I cannot escape. Do not make the same mis-take. I beg of you . . ." Mr. Aquila glanced at his wrist-watch and leaped up. The sprightly returned to his man-ner. "Jeez. It's late. Time to make up your mind, old bourbon and soda. Which will it be? Old face or pretty face? The reality of dreams or the dream of reality?"

"How many decisions did you say we have to make in a lifetime?"

"Five million two hundred and seventy-one thousand and nine. Give or take a thousand. God damn."

"And which one is this for me?"

"Ah? Vérité sans peur. The two million six hundred and thirty-five thousand five hundred and fourth . . . off hand."

"But it's the big one."

"They are all big." Mr. Aquila stepped to the door, placed his hand on the buttons of a rather complicated switch and cocked an eye at Halsyon.

"Voilà tout," he said. "It rests with you."

"I'll take it the hard way," Halsyon decided.

There was a silver chime from the switch, a fizzing aura, a soundless explosion, and Jeffrey Halsyon was ready for his 2,635,505th decision.

Travel Diary

By the end of the Twenty-second century, and at a cost of lives and money exceeding that of the final World War, communication between the planets of the solar system was finally established.

History of Solar Cities
John W. Lackland

June 10. Venus. Staying at the Excelsior. Everybody speaks English so no trouble at all. But they simply have *no* idea how to make Martinis. Nuisance. Went to that marvelous dressmaker Linda told me about. Bought five *divine* creations for practically peanuts. Tom said: "Exchange favors us." I said: "What means?" Tom: "Our dollars buy more here than home." Self: "Then why can't buy six gowns?" Tom: "Doesn't favor us *that* much." But I notice he bought another camera. Pig!

Ran into the Trumbulls and the Rogers. Took us to a marvelous bistro where Clyde Pippin from the old Key Club is playing. Love his songs. Love that man. Tom too embarrassing adding up check with pencil. It's true they all cheat us, but why can't he show them we don't give a D—— Mars and Saturn next. Then Alpha Centaurus.

Speed was the one barrier to practical communication with the planetary systems of the far stars. When faster-than-light propulsion was at last developed after centuries of research, it became possible to travel to the far stars within weeks rather than years.

Development of Galactic Travel
Ezra Coudert

July 19. Alpha Centaurus. Staying at the Excelsior. Everybody speaks English so no trouble at all. But can't drink the water. Nuisance. Went to that marvelous lace man Linda told me about. Bought five yards for practically peanuts.

People here too dirty and positively amoral. Disgusting.

110

And rude? ! ! ! ! Tom took pictures of some kind of silly ceremony. People began screaming at us. Tried to steal T's camera. Official came along and jabbered in broken English. "They say no more take, please. Break." Tom: "Break what?" Official: "Religious. Sacred. No take look-see. Break." Tom: "You got the nerve to tell me that clowning is religion?" Official: "Yes, please." (Pointing to camera) "Give, please. Must break please." Tom: (to me) "How about that for nerve? Give them my four-hundred-dollar camera to bust just because it's taken a few religious pictures." Self: "If it's good enough for Notre Dame, it's good enough for them." Tom gave them some money and we left.

Ran into the Trumbulls and Rogers. Took them to a marvelous bistro where Clyde Pippin is playing now. Made me homesick to hear the old Key Klub tunes. Love that man. Tom too funny pretending to be visiting dignitary. Said was famous Senator from Saturn. Said was here *investigating*. Scared them all to death. Laugh? I tho't I'd die! Betelgeuse next.

> *Conflicting cultures brought about inevitable clashes which culminated in the Great Galactic War. Betelgeuse, bankrupt and desperate, attempted a costly and controversial experiment. The government was overthrown and a one-party business despotism established under the leadership of an economic dictator.*
>
> The Political Economy of Space
> *Arthur Raskober*

July 23. Betelgeuse. Staying at the Excelsior. Everybody speaks English, so very convenient. Can't understand talk about poverty and shortages here. Not true. Food marvelous. Plenty cream, butter, eggs, etc., here in hotel. Not true about unhappiness. All waiters, maids, etc. in hotel cheerful and smiling. And Mudinna certainly has made the planes run on time.

Went to that marvelous beautician Linda told me about. Took all my courage in both hands and *cut my hair*. Tres chic but was afraid to show Tom. When he finally saw, furious! ! ! Said made me look like a d—ed foreigner. He'll get used to it.

Ran into the Trumbulls and Rogers. We all went to a marvelous bistro where Clyde Pippin is playing. Love that man! After two months travel finally became cos-

mopolitan enough to introduce myself to him. Something
would never have dared before. Now, was tremendously
poised. Said: "Mr. Pippin, admired you for twenty years.
Ever since was child." He: "Thanks honey." Self: "Always *adored* the way you sang *Tree Top*." He: "No,
that's Charley Hoyt's number. I never sing it, honey."
Self: "Well I never asked Charley Hoyt for his autograph,
but I'm asking *you*." I was too sophisticated.

Leave for Andromeda tomorrow. Very excited. Will be
high spot of entire trip.

> *Perhaps the most amazing incident in the course
> of the exploration of space was the discovery that
> time-travel had already been developed in Andro-
> meda. Permission for limited use by scientists, histor-
> ians and students was granted in 2754.*
>
> The Exploration of Time
> *Stark Robinson*

August 1. Andromeda. Staying at the Excelsior. Everybody speaks English divinely. Tom and self to authorities
armed with letters from Chamber of Commerce, N.A.M.,
Senator Wilkins, and Joe Cates whose nephew practically
runs the State Dept. We wanted time-trip. They said no,
not for tourists. Too expensive, only for study. Tom finally laid down the law, told a few lies and made a few
threats. They said yes. You have to be firm with these
eggheads.

Tom picked Sept. 5, 1665 in London. Self: "Why?"
Tom: "Because is date of Great Fire that destroyed London. Always dreamed about. Always wanted to see.:
Self: "Don't be childish. A fire's a fire. Want to see Marie
Antionette's clothes." Tom: "No. I swung it. So we see
what *I* want." Selfish! Had to exchange money for Seventeenth century money. Had to wear old Seventeenth century clothes. Not properly cleaned, I tho't. Almost didn't
go.

Was right. Fire is just a fire. But bought some *heavenly*
silver and china and ten place-settings of *divine* flatware.
Also tea set. Tom couldn't complain for once. *He* bought
six swords and a helmet for the rumpus room decorations. Funniest thing about the trip is fact that we could
hardly understand the people there. In 1665 they couldn't
speak their own English.

Next week, home!

Faster-than-light speed while travelling through the universe produces a physical paradox. Although the traveller is conscious of the passage of time within the space ship (Subjective Time), actually he is being transported so rapidly that the trip seems to have taken no time at all to the rest of the world. (Objective Time). In other words, a space ship leaves Andromeda on August 1, bound for earth. It is August 1 when the ship arrives. No time has elapsed in the universe. But on board the ship, travelling at faster-than-light speed, seven days have elapsed.

Paradoxes of Space Travel
Oliver Nielson

August 20. Home. Although is August 20 in this diary, is actually only June 14 here on earth. Can *not* get used to Subj. and Obj. time. Have been gone three months by our counting, but only 14 days by earth's counting. Hate this. Makes me feel as if I'd never left home.

Distributed all gifts we brought back. Linda was imposs. Insists she told me get her a Shocking Pink peignoir on Callisto. Not Powder Blue. That's a D——ed lie and she knows it. She can't wear Shocking with *her* hair. Tom furious. Forgot to take lens cap off new camera when photographing Great Fire. All pictures blank. Now nobody believes he was important enough to wangle time-trip.

The Trumbulls and the Rogers called. Want us to get together and have reunion. Suggested the new Kolony Klub. Clyde Pippin there with his marvelous act. Dying to go, but had to refuse. Too exhausted. The universe is a great place to visit, but I'd sure hate to live there.

✳

Fondly Fahrenheit

HE DOESN'T KNOW WHICH OF US WE ARE THESE DAYS, but they know one truth. You must own nothing but yourself. You must make your own life, live your own life and die your own death . . . or else you will die another's.

The rice fields on Paragon III stretch for hundreds of miles like checkerboard tundras, a blue and brown mosaic under a burning sky of orange. In the evening, clouds whip like smoke, and the paddies rustle and murmur.

A long line of men marched across the paddies the evening we escaped from Paragon III. They were silent, armed, intent; a long rank of silhouetted statues looming against the smoking sky. Each man carried a gun. Each man wore a walkie-talkie belt pack, the speaker button in his ear, the microphone bug clipped to his throat, the glowing view-screen strapped to his wrist like a green-eyed watch. The multitude of screens showed nothing but a multitude of individual paths through the paddies. The annunciators made no sound but the rustle and splash of steps. The men spoke infrequently, in heavy grunts, all speaking to all.

"Nothing here."

"Where's here?"

"Jenson's fields."

"You're drifting too far west."

"Close in the line there."

"Anybody covered the Grimson paddy?"

"Yeah. Nothing."

"She couldn't have walked this far."

"Could have been carried."

"Think she's alive?"

"Why should she be dead?"

The slow refrain swept up and down the long line of beaters advancing toward the smoky sunset. The line of beaters wavered like a writhing snake, but never ceased its remorseless advance. One hundred men spaced fifty feet apart. Five thousand feet of ominous search. One mile of angry determination stretching from east to west across a compass of heart. Evening fell. Each man lit his search lamp. The writhing snake was transformed into a necklace of wavering diamonds.

"Clear here. Nothing."

"Nothing here."

"Nothing."

"What about the Allen paddies?"

"Covering them now."

"Think we missed her?"

"Maybe."

"We'll beat back and check."

"This'll be an all-night job."

"Allen paddies clear."

"God damn! We've got to find her!"

"We'll find her."

"Here she is. Sector seven. Tune in."

The line stopped. The diamonds froze in the heat. There was silence. Each man gazed into the glowing green screen on his wrist, tuning to sector seven. All tuned to one. All showed a small nude figure awash in the muddy water of a paddy. Alongside the figure an owner's stake of bronze read: VANDALEUR. The ends of the line converged toward the Vandaleur field. The necklace turned into a cluster of stars. One hundred men gathered around a small nude body, a child dead in a rice paddy. There was no water in her mouth. There were finger-marks on her throat. Her innocent face was battered. Her body was torn. Clotted blood on her skin was crusted and hard.

"Dead three-four hours at least."

"Her mouth is dry."

"She wasn't drowned. Beaten to death."

In the dark evening heat the men swore softly. They picked up the body. One stopped the others and pointed to the child's fingernails. She had fought her murderer. Under the nails were particles of flesh and bright drops of scarlet blood, still liquid, still uncoagulated.

"That blood ought to be clotted too."

"Funny."

"Not so funny. What kind of blood don't clot?"

"Android."

"Looks like she was killed by one."

"Vandaleur owns an android."

"She couldn't be killed by an android."

"That's android blood under her nails."

"The police better check."

"The police'll prove I'm right."

"But androids can't kill."

"That's android blood, ain't it?"

"Androids can't kill. They're made that way."

"Looks like one android was made wrong."

"Jesus!"

And the thermometer that day registered 92.9° gloriously Fahrenheit.

So there we were aboard the *Paragon Queen* enroute

for Megaster V, James Vandaleur and his android. James
Vandaleur counted his money and wept. In the second-
class cabin with him was his android, a magnificent synthetic creature with classic features and wide blue eyes.
Raised on its forehead in a cameo of flesh were the letters
MA, indicating that this was one of the rare multiple
aptitude androids, worth fifty-seven-thousand dollars on
the current exchange. There we were, weeping and counting and calmly watching.

"Twelve, fourteen, sixteen. Sixteen hundred dollars,"
Vandaleur wept. "That's all. Sixteen hundred dollars. My
house was worth ten thousand. The land was worth five.
There was furniture, cars, my paintings, etchings, my
plane, my— And nothing to show for everything but sixteen hundred dollars. Christ!"

I leaped up from the table and turned on the android.
I pulled a strap from one of the leather bags and beat
the android. It didn't move.

"I must remind you," the android said, "that I am
worth fifty-seven thousand dollars on the current exchange. I must warn you that you are endangering valuable property."

"You damned crazy machine," Vandaleur shouted.

"I am not a machine," the android answered. "The
robot is a machine. The android is a chemical creation
of synthetic tissue."

"What got into you?" Vandaleur cried. "Why did you
do it? Damn you!" He beat the android savagely.

"I must remind you that I cannot be punished," It said.
"The pleasure-pain syndrome is not incorporated in the
android synthesis."

"Then why did you kill her?" Vandaleur shouted. "If
it wasn't for kicks, why did you—"

"I must remind you," the android said, "that the second-class cabins in these ships are not soundproofed."

Vandaleur dropped the strap and stood panting, staring at the creature he owned.

"Why did you do it? Why did you kill her?" I asked.

"I don't know," I answered.

"First it was malicious mischief. Small things. Petty destruction. I should have known there was something
wrong with you then. Androids can't destroy. They can't
harm. They—"

"There is no pleasure-pain syndrome incorporated in
the android synthesis."

"Then it got to arson. Then serious destruction. Then assault . . . that engineer on Rigel. Each time worse. Each time we had to get out faster. Now it's murder. Christ! What's the matter with you? What's happened?"

"There are no self-check relays incorporated in the android brain."

"Each time we had to get out it was a step downhill. Look at me. In a second-class cabin. Me. James Paleologue Vandaleur. There was a time when my father was the wealthiest— Now, sixteen hundred dollars in the world. That's all I've got. And you. Christ damn you!"

Vandaleur raised the strap to beat the android again, then dropped it and collapsed on a berth, sobbing. At last he pulled himself together.

"Instructions," he said.

The multiple aptitude android responded at once. It arose and awaited orders.

"My name is now Valentine. James Valentine. I stopped off on Paragon III for only one day to transfer to this ship for Megaster V. My occupation: Agent for one privately owned MA android which is for hire. Purpose of visit: To settle on Megaster V. Forge the papers."

The android removed Vandaleur's passport and papers from a bag, got pen and ink and sat down at the table. With an accurate, flawless hand—an accomplished hand that could draw, write, paint, carve, engrave, etch, photograph, design, create and build—it meticulously forged new credentials for Vandaleur. Its owner watched me miserably.

"Create and build," I muttered. "And now destroy. Oh, God! What am I going to do? Christ! If I could only get rid of you. If I didn't have to live off you. God! If only I'd inherited some guts instead of you."

Dallas Brady was Megaster's leading jewelry designer. She was short, stocky, amoral and a nymphomaniac. She hired Valentine's multiple aptitude android and put me to work in her shop. She seduced Valentine. In her bed one night, she asked abruptly: "Your name's Vandaleur, isn't it?"

"Yes," I murmured. Then: "No! No! It's Valentine. James Valentine."

"What happened on Paragon?" Dallas Brady asked. "I thought androids couldn't kill or destroy property. Prime Directives and Inhibitions set up for them when they're synthesized. Every company guarantees they can't."

"Valentine!" Vandaleur insisted.

"Oh, come off it," Dallas Brady said. "I've known for a week. I haven't hollered copper, have I?"

"The name is Valentine."

"You want to prove it? You want I should call the police?" Dallas reached out and picked up the phone.

"For God's sake, Dallas!" Vandaleur leaped up and struggled to take the phone from her. She fended him off, laughing at him, until he collapsed and wept in shame and helplessness.

"How did you find out?" he asked at last.

"The papers are full of it. And Valentine was a little too close to Vandaleur. That wasn't smart, was it?"

"I guess not. I'm not very smart."

"Your android's got quite a record, hasn't it? Assault. Arson. Destruction. What happened on Paragon?"

"It kidnaped a child. Took her out into the rice fields and murdered her."

"Raped her?"

"I don't know."

"They're going to catch up with you."

"Don't I know it? Christ! We've been running for two years now. Seven planets in two years. I must have abandoned a hundred thousand dollars worth of property in two years."

"You better find out what's wrong with it."

"How can I? Can I walk into a repair clinic and ask for an overhaul? What am I going to say? 'My android's just turned killer. Fix it.' They'd call the police right off." I began to shake. "They'd have that android dismantled inside one day. I'd probably be booked as accessory to murder."

"Why didn't you have it repaired before it got to murder?"

"I couldn't take the chance," Vandaleur explained angrily. "If they started fooling around with lobotomies and body chemistry and endocrine surgery, they might have destroyed its aptitudes. What would I have left to hire out? How would I live?"

"You could work yourself. People do."

"Work at what? You know I'm good for nothing. How could I compete with specialist androids and robots? Who can, unless he's got a terrific talent for a particular job?"

"Yeah. That's true."

"I lived off my old man all my life. Damn him! He had to go bust just before he died. Left me the android and that's all. The only way I can get along is living off what it earns."

"You better sell it before the cops catch up with you. You can live off fifty grand. Invest it."

"At 3 per cent? Fifteen hundred a year? When the android returns 15 per cent on its value? Eight thousand a year. That's what it earns. No, Dallas. I've got to go along with it."

"What are you going to do about its violence kick?"

"I can't do anything . . . except watch it and pray. What are you going to do about it?"

"Nothing. It's none of my business. Only one thing . . . I ought to get something for keeping my mouth shut."

"What?"

"The android works for me for free. Let somebody else pay you, but I get it for free."

The multiple aptitude android worked. Vandaleur collected its fees. His expenses were taken care of. His savings began to mount. As the warm spring of Megaster V turned to hot summer, I began investigating farms and properties. It would be possible, within a year or two, for us to settle down permanently, provided Dallas Brady's demands did not become rapacious.

On the first hot day of summer, the android began singing in Dallas Brady's workshop. It hovered over the electric furnace which, along with the weather, was broiling the shop, and sang an ancient tune that had been popular half a century before.

> Oh, it's no feat to beat the heat.
> All reet! All reet!
> So jeet your seat
> Be fleet be fleet
> Cool and discreet
> Honey . . .

It sang in a strange, halting voice, and its accomplished fingers were clasped behind its back, writhing in a strange rumba all their own. Dallas Brady was surprised.

"You happy or something?" she asked.

"I must remind you that the pleasure-pain syndrome is not incorporated in the android synthesis," I answered.

"All reet! All reet! Be fleet be fleet, cool and discreet, honey . . ."

Its fingers stopped their twisting and picked up a heavy pair of iron tongs. The android poked them into the glowing heart of the furnace, leaning far forward to peer into the lovely heat.

"Be careful, you damned fool!" Dallas Brady exclaimed. "You want to fall in?"

"I must remind you that I am worth fifty-seven thousand dollars on the current exchange," I said. "It is forbidden to endanger valuable property. All reet! All reet! Honey . . ."

It withdrew a crucible of glowing gold from the electric furnace, turned, capered hideously, sang crazily, and splashed a sluggish gobbet of molten gold over Dallas Brady's head. She screamed and collapsed, her hair and clothes flaming, her skin crackling. The android poured again while it capered and sang.

"Be fleet be fleet, cool and discreet, honey . . ." It sang and slowly poured and poured the molten gold until the writhing body was still. Then I left the workshop and rejoined James Vandaleur in his hotel suite. The android's charred clothes and squirming fingers warned its owner that something was very much wrong.

Vandaleur rushed to Dallas Brady's workshop, stared once, vomited and fled. I had enough time to pack one bag and raise nine hundred dollars on portable assets. He took a third class cabin on the *Megaster Queen* which left that morning for Lyra Alpha. He took me with him. He wept and counted his money and I beat the android again.

And the thermometer in Dallas Brady's workshop registered 98.1° beautifully Fahrenheit.

On Lyra Alpha we holed up in a small hotel near the university. There, Vandaleur carefully bruised my forehead until the letters MA were obliterated by the swelling and the discoloration. The letters would reappear again, but not for several months, and in the meantime Vandaleur hoped the hue and cry for an MA android would be forgotten. The android was hired out as a common laborer in the university power plant. Vandaleur, as James Venice, eked out life on the android's small earnings.

I wasn't too unhappy. Most of the other residents in the hotel were university students, equally hard up, but delightfully young and enthusiastic. There was one charming girl with sharp eyes and a quick mind. Her name was Wanda, and she and her beau, Jed Stark, took a tremendous interest in the killing android which was being mentioned in every paper in the galaxy.

"We've been studying the case," she and Jed said at one of the casual student parties which happened to be held this night in Vandaleur's room. "We think we know what's causing it. We're going to do a paper." They were in a high state of excitement.

"Causing what?" somebody wanted to know.

"The android rampage."

"Obviously out of adjustment, isn't it? Body chemistry gone haywire. Maybe a kind of synthetic cancer, yes?"

"No." Wanda gave Jed a look of suppressed triumph.

"Well, what is it?"

"Something specific."

"What?"

"That would be telling."

"Oh, come on."

"Nothing doing."

"Won't you tell us?" I asked intently. "I . . . We're very much interested in what could go wrong with an android."

"No, Mr. Venice," Wanda said. "It's a unique idea and we've got to protect it. One thesis like this and we'll be set up for life. We can't take the chance of somebody stealing it."

"Can't you give us a hint?"

"No. Not a hint. Don't say a word, Jed. But I'll tell you this much, Mr. Venice. I'd hate to be the man who owns that android."

"You mean the police?" I asked.

"I mean projection, Mr. Venice. Psychotic projection! That's the danger . . . and I won't say any more. I've said too much as is."

I heard steps outside, and a hoarse voice singing softly: "Be fleet be fleet, cool and discreet, honey . . ." My android entered the room, home from its tour of duty at the university power plant. It was not introduced. I motioned to it and I immediately responded to the command and went to the beer keg and took over Vandaleur's job of serving the guests. Its accomplished fingers writhed in a private rumba of their own. Gradually they stopped their squirming, and the strange humming ended.

Androids were not unusual at the university. The wealthier students owned them along with cars and planes. Vandaleur's android provoked no comment, but young Wanda was sharp-eyed and quick-witted. She noted my bruised forehead and she was intent on the history-making thesis she and Jed Stark were going to write. After the party broke up, she consulted with Jed walking upstairs to her room.

"Jed, why'd that android have a bruised forehead?"

"Probably hurt itself, Wanda. It's working in the power plant. They fling a lot of heavy stuff around."

"That all?"

"What else?"

"It could be a convenient bruise."

"Convenient for what?"

"Hiding what's stamped on its forehead."

"No point to that, Wanda. You don't have to see marks on a forehead to recognize an android. You don't have to see a trademark on a car to know it's a car."

"I don't mean it's trying to pass as a human. I mean it's trying to pass as a lower grade android."

"Why?"

"Suppose it had MA on its forehead."

"Multiple aptitude? Then why in hell would Venice waste it stoking furnaces if it could earn more—Oh. Oh! You mean it's—?"

Wanda nodded.

"Jesus! Stark pursed his lips. "What do we do? Call the police?"

"No. We don't know if it's an MA for a fact. If it turns out to be an MA and the killing android, our paper comes first anyway. This is our big chance, Jed. If it's *that* android we can run a series of controlled tests and—"

"How do we find out for sure?"

"Easy. Infrared film. That'll show what's under the bruise. Borrow a camera. We'll sneak down to the power plant tomorrow afternoon and take some pictures. Then we'll know."

They stole down into the university power plant the following afternoon. It was a vast cellar, deep under the earth. It was dark, shadowy, luminous with burning light from the furnace doors. Above the roar of the fires they could hear a strange voice shouting and chanting in the echoing vault: "All reet! All reet! So jeet your seat. Be fleet be fleet, cool and discreet, honey . . ." And they could see a capering figure dancing a lunatic rhumba in time to the music it shouted. The legs twisted. The arms waved. The fingers writhed.

Jed Stark raised the camera and began shooting his spool of infrared film, aiming the camera sights at that bobbing head. Then Wanda shrieked, for I saw them and came charging down on them, brandishing a polished steel shovel. It smashed the camera. It felled the girl and then the boy. Jed fought me for a desperate hissing moment before he was bludgeoned into helplessness. Then the android dragged them to the furnace and fed them to the flames, slowly, hideously. It capered and sang. Then it returned to my hotel.

The thermometer in the power plant registered 100.9° murderously Fahrenheit. All reet! All reet!

We bought steerage on the *Lyra Queen* and Vandaleur and the android did odd jobs for their meals. During the night watches, Vandaleur would sit alone in the steerage head with a cardboard portfolio on his lap, puzzling over its contents. That portfolio was all he had managed to bring with him from Lyra Alpha. He had stolen it from Wanda's room. It was labeled ANDROID. It contained the secret of my sickness.

And it contained nothing but newspapers. Scores of newspapers from all over the galaxy, printed, microfilmed, engraved, etched, offset, photostated . . . Rigel *Star-Banner* . . . Paragon *Picayune* . . . Megaster *Times-Leader* . . . Lalande *Herald* . . . Lacaille *Journal* . . . Indi *Intelligencer* . . . Eridani *Telegram-News*. All reet! All reet!

Nothing but newspapers. Each paper contained an account of one crime in the android's ghastly career. Each paper also contained news, domestic and foreign, sports, society, weather, shipping news, stock exchange quotations, human interest stories, features, contests, puzzles. Somewhere in that mass of uncollated facts was the secret Wanda and Jed Stark had discovered. Vandaleur pored over the papers helplessly. It was beyond him. So jeet your seat!

"I'll sell you," I told the android. "Damn you. When we land on Terra, I'll sell you. I'll settle for 3 per cent on whatever you're worth."

"I am worth fifty-seven thousand dollars on the current exchange," I told him.

"If I can't sell you, I'll turn you in to the police," I said.

"I am valuable property," I answered. "It is forbidden to endanger valuable property. You won't have me destroyed."

"Christ damn you!" Vandaleur cried. "What? Are you arrogant? Do you know you can trust me to protect you? Is that the secret?"

The multiple aptitude android regarded him with calm accomplished eyes. "Sometimes," it said, "it is a good thing to be property."

It was three below zero when the *Lyra Queen* dropped at Croydon Field. A mixture of ice and snow swept across the field, fizzing and exploding into steam under the *Queen's* tail jets. The passengers trotted numbly across the blackened concrete to customs inspection, and thence to the airport bus that was to take them to London. Vandaleur and the android were broke. They walked.

By midnight they reached Piccadilly Circus. The December ice storm had not slackened and the statue of Eros was encrusted with ice. They turned right, walked down to Trafalgar Square and then along the Strand, shaking with cold and wet. Just above Fleet Street, Vandaleur saw a solitary figure coming from the direction of St. Paul's. He drew the android into an alley.

"We've got to have money," he whispered. He pointed to the approaching figure. "He has money. Take it from him."

"The order cannot be obeyed." The android said.

"Take it from him," Vandaleur repeated. "By force. Do you understand? We're desperate."

"It is contrary to my prime directive," the android repeated. "The order cannot be obeyed."

"Damn you!" I said. "You've murdered . . . tortured . . . destroyed! You tell me that *now?*"

"It is forbidden to endanger life or property. The order cannot be obeyed."

I thrust the android back and leaped out at the stranger. He was tall, austere, poised. He had an air of hope curdled by cynicism. He carried a cane. I saw he was blind.

"Yes?" he said. "I hear you near me. What is it?"

"Sir . . ." Vandaleur hesitated. "I'm desperate."

"We are all desperate," the stranger replied. "Quietly desperate."

"Sir . . . I've got to have some money."

"Are you begging or stealing?" The sightless eyes passed over Vandaleur and the android.

"I'm prepared for either."

"Ah. So are we all. It is the history of our race." The stranger motioned over his shoulder. "I have been begging at St. Paul's, my friend. What I desire cannot be stolen. What is it you desire that you are lucky enough to be able to steal?"

"Money," Vandaleur said.

"Money for what? Come, my friend, let us exchange confidences. I will tell you why I beg, if you will tell me why you steal. My name is Blenheim."

"My name is . . . Vole."

"I was not begging for sight at St. Paul's, Mr. Vole. I was begging for a number."

"A number?"

"Ah yes. Numbers rational, numbers irrational. Numbers imaginary. Positive integers. Negative integers. Fractions, positive and negative. Eh? You have never heard of Blenheim's immortal treatise on Twenty Zeros, or The Differences in Absence of Quantity? Blenheim smiled bitterly. "I am the wizard of the Theory of Number, Mr. Vole, and I have exhausted the charm of Number for myself. After fifty years of wizardy, senility approaches and the appetite vanishes. I have been praying in St. Paul's for inspiration. Dear God, I prayed, if You exist, send me a Number."

Vandaleur slowly lifted the cardboard portfolio and touched Blenheim's hand with it. "In here," he said, "is a number. A hidden number. A secret number. The number of a crime. Shall we exchange, Mr. Blenheim? Shelter for a number?"

"Neither begging nor stealing, eh?" Blenheim said. "But a bargain. So all life reduces itself to the banal." The sightless eyes again passed over Vandaleur and the android. "Perhaps the Almighty is not God but a merchant. Come home with me."

On the top floor of Blenheim's house we shared a room —two beds, two closets, two washstands, one bathroom. Vandaleur bruised my forehead again and sent me out to find work, and while the android worked, I consulted with Blenheim and read him the papers from the portfolio, one by one. All reet! All reet!

Vandaleur told him this much and no more. He was a
student, I said, planning a thesis on the murdering android. In these papers which he had collected were the
facts that would explain the crimes of which Blenheim
had heard nothing. There must be a correlation, a number, a statistic, something which would account for my
derangement, I explained, and Blenheim was piqued by
the mystery, the detective story, the human interest of
Number.

We examined the papers. As I read them aloud, he
listed them and their contents in his blind, meticulous
writing. And then I read his notes to him. He listed the
papers by type, by type-face, by fact, by fancy, by ar-
ticle, spelling, words, theme, advertising, pictures, subject, politics, prejudices. He analyzed. He studied. He
meditated. And we lived together in that top floor, always
a little cold, always a little terrified, always a little closer
. . . brought together by our fear of us, our hatred between us driven like a wedge into a living tree and splitting the trunk, only to be forever incorporated into the
scar tissue. So we grew together; Vandaleur and the android. Be fleet be fleet.

And one afternoon Blenheim called Vandaleur into
his study and displayed his notes. "I think I've found it,"
he said, "but I can't understand it."

Vandaleur's heart leaped.

"Here are the correlations," Blenheim continued. "In
fifty papers there are accounts of the criminal android.
What is there, outside the depredations, that is also in
fifty papers?"

"I don't know, Mr. Blenheim."

"It was a rhetorical question. Here is the answer. The
weather."

"What?"

"The weather." Blenheim nodded. "Each crime was
committed on a day when the temperature was above
ninety degrees Fahrenheit."

"But that's impossible," Vandaleur exclaimed. "It was
cold at the university on Lyra Alpha."

"We have no record of any crime committed on Lyra
Alpha. There is no paper."

"No. That's right. I—" Vandaleur was confused. Sud-
denly he exclaimed. "No. You're right. The furnace room.
It was hot down there. Hot! Of course. My God, yes!
That's the answer. Dallas Brady's electric furnace . . . The

rice deltas on Paragon. So jeet your seat. Yes. But why? Why? My God, why?"

I came into the house at that moment and, passing the study, saw Vandaleur and Blenheim. I entered, awaiting commands, my multiple aptitudes devoted to service.

"That's the android, eh?" Blenheim said after a long moment.

"Yes," Vandaleur answered, still confused by the discovery. "And that explains why it refused to attack you that night on the Strand. It wasn't hot enough to break the prime directive. Only in the heat . . . The heat, all reet!" He looked at the android. A lunatic command passed from man to android. I refused. It is forbidden to endanger life. Vandaleur gestured furiously, then seized Blenheim's shoulders and yanked him back out of his desk chair to the floor. Blenheim shouted once. Vandaleur leaped on him like a tiger, pinning him to the floor and sealing his mouth with one hand.

"Find a weapon," I called to the android.

"It is forbidden to endanger life."

"This is a fight for self-preservation. Bring me a weapon!" He held the squirming mathematician with all his weight. I went at once to a cupboard where I knew a revolver was kept. I checked it. It was loaded with five cartridges. I handed it to Vandaleur. I took it, rammed the barrel against Blenheim's head and pulled the trigger. He shuddered once.

We had three hours before the cook returned from her day off. We looted the house. We took Blenheim's money and jewels. We packed a bag with clothes. We took Blenheim's notes, destroyed the newspapers, and we fled, carefully locking the door behind us. In Blenheim's study we left a pile of crumpled papers under a half inch of burning candle. And we soaked the rug around it with kerosene. No, I did all that. The android refused. I am forbidden to endanger life or property.

All reet!

They took the tubes to Leicester Square, changed trains and rode to the British Museum. There they got off and went to a small Georgian house just off Russell Square. A shingle in the window read: NAN WEBB, PSYCHOMETRIC CONSULTANT. Vandaleur had made a note of the address some weeks earlier. They went into the house. The android waited in the foyer with the bag. Vandaleur entered Nan Webb's office.

She was a tall woman with gray shingled hair, very
fine English complexion and very bad English legs. Her
features were blunt, her expression acute. She nodded to
Vandaleur, finished a letter, sealed it and looked up.

"My name," I said, "is Vanderbilt. James Vanderbilt."

"Quite."

"I'm an exchange student at London University."

"Quite."

"I've been researching on the killing android, and I
think I've discovered something very interesting. I'd like
your advice on it. What is your fee?"

"What is your college at the university?"

"Why?"

"There is a discount for students."

"Merton College."

"That will be two pounds, please."

Vandaleur placed two pounds on the desk and added
to the fee Blenheim's notes. "There is a correlation," he
said, "between the crimes of the android and the weather.
You will note that each crime was committed when the
temperature rose above ninety degrees Fahrenheit. Is there
a psychometric answer for this?"

Nan Webb nodded, studied the notes for a moment,
put down the sheets of paper and said: "Synesthesia, obviously."

"What?"

"Synesthesia," she repeated. "When a sensation, Mr.
Vanderbilt, is interpreted immediately in terms of a sensation from a different sense organ than the one stimulated, it is called synesthesia. For example: A sound
stimulus gives rise to a simultaneous sensation of definite
color. Or color gives rise to a sensation of taste. Or a
light stimulus gives rise to a sensation of sound. There
can be confusion or short circuiting of any sensation of
taste, smell, pain pressure, temperature and so on. D'you
understand?"

"I think so."

"Your research has uncovered the fact that the android
most probably reacts to temperature stimulus above the
ninety-degree level synesthetically. Most probably there
is an endocrine response. Probably a temperature linkage
with the android adrenal surrogate. High temperature
brings about a response of fear, anger, excitement and
violent physical activity . . . all within the province of
the adrenal gland."

"Yes. I see. Then if the android were to be kept in cold climates . . ."

"There would be neither stimulus nor response. There would be no crimes. Quite."

"I see. What is Psychotic projection?"

"How do you mean?"

"Is there any danger of projection with regard to the owner of the android?"

"Very interesting. Projection is a throwing forward. It is the process of throwing out upon another the ideas or impulses that belong to oneself. The paranoid, for example, projects upon others his conflicts and disturbances in order to externalize them. He accuses, directly or by implication, other men of having the very sicknesses with which he is struggling himself."

"And the danger of projection?"

"It is the danger of the victim's believing what is implied. If you live with a psychotic who projects his sickness upon you, there is a danger of falling into his psychotic pattern and becoming virtually psychotic yourself. As, no doubt, is happening to you, Mr. Vandaleur."

Vandaleur leaped to his feet.

"You are an ass," Nan Webb went on crisply. She waved the sheets of notes. "This is no exchange student's writing. It's the unique cursive of the famous Blenheim. Every scholar in England knows this blind writing. There is no Merton College at London University. That was a miserable guess. Merton is one of the Oxford Colleges. And you, Mr. Vandaleur, are so obviously infected by association with your deranged android . . . by projection, if you will . . . that I hesitate between calling the Metropolitan Police and the Hospital for the Criminally Insane."

I took the gun out and shot her.

Reet!

"Antares II, Alpha Aurigae, Acrux IV, Pollux IX, Rigel Centaurus," Vandaleur said. "They're all cold. Cold as a witch's kiss. Mean temperatures of forty degrees Fahrenheit. Never get hotter than seventy. We're in business again. Watch that curve."

The multiple aptitude android swung the wheel with its accomplished hands. The car took the curve sweetly and sped on through the northern marshes, the reeds stretching for miles, brown and dry, under the cold English sky. The sun was sinking swiftly. Overhead, a lone flight of bustards flapped clumsily eastward. High above the flight, a lone helicopter drifted toward home and warmth.

"No more warmth for us," I said. "No more heat. We're safe when we're cold. We'll hole up in Scotland, make a little money, get across to Norway, build a bankroll and then ship out. We'll settle on Pollux. We're safe. We've licked it. We can live again."

There was a startling *bleep* from overhead, and then a ragged roar: "ATTENTION JAMES VANDALEUR AND ANDROID. ATTENTION JAMES VANDALEUR AND ANDROID."

Vandaleur started and looked up. The lone helicopter was floating above them. From its belly came amplified commands: "YOU ARE SURROUNDED. THE ROAD IS BLOCKED. YOU ARE TO STOP YOUR CAR AT ONCE AND SUBMIT TO ARREST. STOP AT ONCE!"

I looked at Vandaleur for orders.

"Keep driving," Vandaleur snapped.

The helicopter dropped lower: "ATTENTION ANDROID. YOU ARE IN CONTROL OF THE VEHICLE. YOU ARE TO STOP AT ONCE. THIS IS A STATE DIRECTIVE SUPERSEDING ALL PRIVATE COMMANDS."

The car slowed.

"What the hell are you doing?" I shouted.

"A state directive supersedes all private commands," the android answered. "I must point out to you that—"

"Get the hell away from the wheel," Vandaleur ordered. I clubbed the android, yanked him sideways and squirmed over him to the wheel. The car veered off the road in that moment and went churning through the frozen mud and dry reeds. Vandaleur regained control and continued westward through the marshes toward a parallel highway five miles distant.

"We'll beat their God damned block," he grunted.

The car pounded and surged. The helicopter dropped even lower. A searchlight blazed from the belly of the plane.

"ATTENTION JAMES VANDALEUR AND ANDROID. SUBMIT TO ARREST. THIS IS A STATE DIRECTIVE SUPERSEDING ALL PRIVATE COMMANDS."

"He can't submit," Vandaleur shouted wildly. "There's no one to submit to. He can't and I won't."

"Christ!" I muttered. "We'll beat them yet. We'll beat the block. We'll beat the heat. We'll—"

"I must point out to you," I said, "that I am required by my prime directive to obey state directives which supersede all private commands. I must submit to arrest."

"Who says it's a state directive?" Vandaleur said. "Them? Up in that plane? They've got to show credentials. They've got to prove it's state authority before you submit. How d'you know they're not crooks trying to trick us?"

Holding the wheel with one arm, he reached into his side pocket to make sure the gun was still in place. The car skidded. The tires squealed on frost and reeds. The wheel was wrenched from his grasp and the car yawed up a small hillock and overturned. The motor roared and the wheels screamed. Vandaleur crawled out and dragged the android with him. For the moment we were outside the cone of light blazing down from the helicopter. We blundered off into the marsh, into the blackness, into concealment . . . Vandaleur running with a pounding heart, hauling the android along.

The helicopter circled and soared over the wrecked car, searchlight peering, loudspeaker braying. On the highway we had left, lights appeared as the pursuing and blocking parties gathered and followed radio directions from the plane. Vandaleur and the android continued deeper and deeper into the marsh, working their way towards the parallel road and safety. It was night by now. The sky was a black matte. Not a star showed. The temperature was dropping. A southeast night wind knifed us to the bone.

Far behind there was a dull concussion. Vandaleur turned, gasping. The car's fuel had exploded. A geyser of flame shot up like a lurid fountain. It subsided into a low crater of burning reeds. Whipped by the wind, the distant hem of flame fanned up into a wall, ten feet high. The wall began marching down on us, crackling fiercely. Above it, a pall of oily smoke surged forward. Behind it, Vandaleur could make out the figures of men . . . a mass of beaters searching the marsh.

"Christ!" I cried and searched desperately for safety. He ran, dragging me with him, until their feet crunched

through the surface ice of a pool. He trampled the ice
furiously, then flung himself down in the numbing water,
pulling the android with us.

The wall of flame approached. I could hear the crackle
and feel the heat. He could see the searchers clearly.
Vandaleur reached into his side pocket for the gun. The
pocket was torn. The gun was gone. He groaned and
shook with cold and terror. The light from the marsh
fire was blinding. Overhead, the helicopter floated helplessly to one side, unable to fly through the smoke and
flames and aid the searchers who were beating far to the
right of us.

"They'll miss us," Vandaleur whispered. "Keep quiet.
That's an order. They'll miss us. We'll beat them. We'll
beat the fire. We'll—"

Three distinct shots sounded less than a hundred feet
from the fugitives. *Blam! Blam! Blam!* They came
from the last three cartridges in my gun as the marsh
fire reached it where it had dropped, and exploded the
shells. The searchers turned toward the sound and began
working directly toward us. Vandaleur cursed hysterically
and tried to submerge even deeper to escape the intolerable heat of the fire. The android began to twitch.

The wall of flame surged up to them. Vandaleur took
a deep breath and prepared to submerge until the flame
passed over them. The android shuddered and suddenly
began to scream.

"All reet! All reet!" it shouted. "Be fleet be fleet!"

"Damn you!" I shouted. I tried to drown the android.
"Damn you!" I cursed. I smashed Vandaleur's face.

The android battered Vandaleur, who fought it off until
it burst out of the mud and staggered upright. Before I
could return to the attack, the live flames captured it
hypnotically. It danced and capered in a lunatic rhumba
before the wall of fire. Its legs twisted. Its arms waved.
The fingers writhed in a private rhumba of their own. It
shrieked and sang and ran in a crooked waltz before
the embrace of the heat, a muddy monster silhouetted
against the brilliant sparkling flare.

The searchers shouted. There were shots. The android
spun around twice and then continued its horrid dance
before the face of the flames. There was a rising gust of
wind. The fire swept around the capering figure and en-
veloped it for a roaring moment. Then the fire swept on,

leaving behind it a sobbing mass of synthetic flesh oozing scarlet blood that would never coagulate.

The thermometer would have registered 1200° wondrously Fahrenheit.

Vandaleur didn't die. I got away. They missed him while they watched the android caper and die. But I don't know which of us he is these days. Psychotic projection, Wanda warned me. Projection, Nan Webb told him. If you live with a crazy machine long enough, I become crazy too. Reet!

But we know one truth. We know they were wrong. It was the other way around. It was the man that was corrupting the machine . . . any machine . . . all machines. The new robot and Vandaleur know that because the new robot's started twitching too. Reet!

Here on cold Pollux, the robot is twitching and singing. No heat, but my fingers writhe. No heat, but it's taken the little Talley girl off for a solitary walk. A cheap labor robot. A servo-mechanism . . . all I could afford . . . but it's twitching and humming and walking alone with the child somewhere and I can't find them. Christ! Vandaleur can't find me before it's too late. Cool and discreet, honey, in the dancing frost while the thermometer registers 10° fondly Fahrenheit.

✳

Hobson's Choice

THIS IS A WARNING TO ACCOMPLICES LIKE YOU, ME, and Addyer.

Can you spare price of one cup coffee, honorable sir? I am indigent organism which are hungering.

By day, Addyer was a statistician. He concerned himself with such matters as Statistical Tables, Averages and Dispersions, Groups That Are Not Homogenous, and Random Sampling. At night, Addyer plunged into an elaborate escape fantasy divided into two parts. Either he imagined himself moved back in time a hundred years with a double armful of the *Encyclopaedia Britannica*, bestsellers, hit plays and gambling records; or else he imagined himself transported forward in time a thousand years to the Golden Age of perfection.

There were other fantasies which Addyer entertained on odd Thursdays, such as (by a fluke) becoming the only man left on earth with a world of passionate beauties to fecundate; such as acquiring the power of invisibility which would enable him to rob banks and right wrongs with impunity; such as possessing the mysterious power of working miracles.

Up to this point you and I and Addyer are identical. Where we part company is in the fact that Addyer was a statistician.

Can you spare cost of one cup coffee, honorable miss? For blessed charitability? I am beholden.

On Monday, Addyer rushed into his chief's office, waving a sheaf of papers. "Look here, Mr. Grande," Addyer sputtered. "I've found something fishy. Extremely fishy . . . In the statistical sense, that is."

"Oh hell," Grande answered. "You're not supposed to be finding anything. We're in between statistics until the war's over."

"I was leafing through the Interior Department's reports. D'you know our population's up?"

"Not after the Atom Bomb it isn't," said Grande. "We've lost double what our birth rate can replace." He pointed out the window to the twenty-five foot stub of the Washington Monument. "There's your documentation."

"But our population's up 3.0915 per cent." Addyer displayed his figures. "What about that, Mr. Grande?"

"Must be a mistake somewhere," Grande muttered after a moment's inspection. "You'd better check."

"Yes, sir," said Addyer scurrying out of the office. "I knew you'd be interested, sir. You're the ideal statistician, sir." He was gone.

"Poop," said Grande and once again began computing the quantity of bored respirations left to him. It was his personalized anesthesia.

On Tuesday, Addyer discovered that there was no correlation between the mortality-birth rate ratio and the population increase. The war was multiplying mortality and reducing births; yet the population was minutely increasing. Addyer displayed his discovery to Grande, received a pat on the back, and went home to a new fantasy in which he woke up a million years in the future, learned the answer to the enigma, and decided to remain amidst snow-capped mountains and snow-capped bosoms, safe under the aegis of a culture saner than aureomycin.

On Wednesday, Addyer requisitioned the comptometer and file and ran a test check on Washington, D.C. To his dismay he discovered that the population of the former capital was down 0.0029 per cent. This was distressing, and Addyer went home to escape into a dream about Queen Victoria's Golden Age where he amazed and confounded the world with his brilliant output of novels, plays and poetry, all cribbed from Shaw, Galsworthy and Wilde.

Can you spare price of one coffee, honorable sir? I am distressed individual needful of chariting.

On Thursday, Addyer tried another check, this time on the city of Philadelphia. He discovered that Philadelphia's population was up 0.0959 per cent. Very encouraging. He tried a run-down on Little Rock. Population up 1.1329 per cent. He tested St. Louis. Population up 2.-0924 per cent . . . and this despite the complete extinction of Jefferson County owing to one of those military mistakes of an excessive nature.

"My God!" Addyer exclaimed, trembling with excitement. "The closer I get to the center of the country, the greater the increase. But it was the center of the country that took the heaviest punishment in the Buz-Raid. What's the answer?"

That night he shuttled back and forth between the future and the past in his ferment, and he was down at the shop by seven A.M. He put a twenty-four hour claim on the Compo and Files. He followed up his hunch and he came up with a fantastic discovery which he graphed in approved form. On the map of the remains of the United States he drew concentric circles in colors illustrating the areas of population increase. The red, orange, yellow, green and blue circles formed a perfect target around Finney County, Kansas.

"Mr. Grande," Addyer shouted in a high statistical passion, "Finney County has got to explain this."

"You go out there and get that explanation," Grande replied, and Addyer departed.

"Poop," muttered Grande and began integrating his pulse-rate with his eye-blink.

*Can you spare price of one coffee, dearly madam?
I am staveling organism requiring nutritiousment.*

Now travel in those days was hazardous. Addyer took ship to Charleston (there were no rail connections remaining in the North Atlantic states) and was wrecked off Hatteras by a rogue mine. He drifted in the icy waters for seventeen hours, muttering through his teeth: "Oh Christ! If only I'd been born a hundred years ago."

Apparently this form of prayer was potent. He was picked up by a Navy Sweeper and shipped to Charleston where he arrived just in time to acquire a sub-critical radiation burn from a raid which fortunately left the railroad unharmed. He was treated for the burn from Charleston to Macon (change) from Birmingham to Memphis (bubonic plague) to Little Rock (polluted water) to Tulsa (fall-out quarantine) to Kansas City (The O.K. Bus Co. Accepts No Liability for Lives Lost Through Acts of War) to Lyoness, Finney County, Kansas.

And there he was in Finney County with its great magma pits and scars and radiation streaks; whole farms blackened and razed; whole highways so blasted they looked like dotted lines; whole population 4-F. Clouds of soot and fall-out neutralizers hung over Finney County by day, turning it into a Pittsburgh on a still afternoon. Auras of radiation glowed at night, high-lighted by the blinking red warning beacons, turning the county into one of those over-exposed night photographs, all blurred and cross-hatched by deadly slashes of light.

After a restless night in Lyonesse Hotel, Addyer went over to the County Seat for a check on their birth records. He was armed with the proper credentials, but the County Seat was not armed with the statistics. That excessive military mistake again. It had extinguished the Seat.

A little annoyed, Addyer marched off to the County Medical Association office. His idea was to poll the local doctors on births. There was an office and one attendant who had been a practical nurse. He informed Addyer that Finney County had lost its last doctor to the army eight months previous. Midwives might be the answer to the birth enigma but there was no record of midwives. Addyer would simply have to canvass from door to door, asking if any lady within practiced that ancient profession.

Further piqued, Addyer returned to the Lyonesse Hotel and wrote on a slip of tissue paper: HAVING DATA DIFFICULTIES. WILL REPORT AS SOON AS INFORMATION AVAILABLE. He slipped the message into an aluminum capsule, attached it to his sole surviving carrier pigeon, and dispatched it to Washington with a prayer. Then he sat down at his window and brooded.

He was aroused by a curious sight. In the street below, the O.K. Bus Co. had just arrived from Kansas City. The old coach wheezed to a stop, opened its door with some difficulty and permitted a one-legged farmer to emerge. His burned face was freshly bandaged. Evidently this was a well-to-do burgess who could afford to travel for medical treatment. The bus backed up for the return trip to Kansas City and honked a warning horn. That was when the curious sight began.

From nowhere . . . absolutely nowhere . . . a horde of people appeared. They skipped from back alleys, from behind rubble piles; they popped out of stores, they filled the street. They were all jolly, healthy, brisk, happy. They laughed and chatted as they climbed into the bus. They looked like hikers and tourists, carrying knapsacks, carpet-bags, box lunches and even babies. In two minutes the bus was filled. It lurched off down the road, and as it disappeared Addyer heard happy singing break out and echo from the walls of rubble.

"I'll be damned," he said.

He hadn't heard spontaneous singing in over two years. He hadn't seen a carefree smile in over three years. He felt like a color-blind man who was seeing the full spectrum for the first time. It was uncanny. It was also a little blasphemous.

"Don't those people know there's a war on?" he asked himself.

And a little later: "They looked too healthy. Why aren't they in uniform?"

And last of all: "Who *were* they anyway?"

That night Addyer's fantasy was confused.

Can you spare price of one cup coffee, kindly sir?
I am estrangered and faintly from hungering.

The next morning Addyer arose early, hired a car at
an exorbitant fee, found he could not buy any fuel at
any price, and ultimately settled for a lame horse. He was
allergic to horse dander and suffered asthmatic tortures
as he began his house-to-house canvass. He was dis-
couraged when he returned to the Lyonesse Hotel that
afternoon. He was just in time to witness the departure
of the O.K. Bus Co.

Once again a horde of happy people appeared and
boarded the bus. Once again the bus hirpled off down the
broken road. Once again the joyous singing broke out.

"I *will* be damned," Addyer wheezed.

He dropped into the County Surveyor's Office for a
large scale map of Finney County. It was his intent to
plot the midwife coverage in accepted statistical manner.
There was a little difficulty with the Surveyor who was
deaf, blind in one eye, and spectacleless in the other.
He could not read Addyer's credentials with any faculty
or facility. As Addyer finally departed with the map, he
said to himself: "I think the old idiot thought I was a
spy."

And later he muttered: "Spies?"

And just before bedtime: "Holy Moses! Maybe *that's*
the answer to *them.*"

That night he was Lincoln's secret agent, anticipating
Lee's every move, outwitting Jackson, Johnston and Beau-
regard, foiling John Wilkes Booth, and being elected President of the United States by 1868.

The next day the O.K. Bus Co. carried off yet another
load of happy people.

And the next.

And the next.

"Four hundred tourists in five days," Addyer computed.
"The country's filled with espionage."

He began loafing around the streets trying to investigate these joyous travellers. It was difficult. They were
elusive before the bus arrived. They had a friendly way
of refusing to pass the time. The locals of Lyonesse knew
nothing about them and were not interested. Nobody was
interested in much more than painful survival these days.
That was what made the singing obscene.

After seven days of cloak-and-dagger and seven days of counting, Addyer suddenly did the big take. "It adds up," he said. "Eighty people a day leaving Lyonesse. Five hundred a week. Twenty-five thousand a year. Maybe that's the answer to the population increase." He spent fifty-five dollars on a telegram to Grande with no more than a hope of delivery. The Telegram read: "EUREKA. I HAVE FOUND (IT)."

Can you spare price of lone cup coffee, honorable madam? I am not tramp-handler but destitute life-form.

Addyer's opportunity came the next day. The O.K. Bus Co. pulled in as usual. Another crowd assembled to board the bus, but this time there were too many. Three people were refused passage. They weren't in the least annoyed. They stepped back, waved energetically as the bus started, shouted instructions for future reunions and then quietly turned and started off down the street.

Addyer was out of his hotel room like a shot. He followed the trio down the main street, turned left after them onto Fourth Avenue, passed the ruined schoolhouse, passed the demolished telephone building, passed the gutted library, railroad station, Protestant Church, Catholic Church . . . and finally reached the outskirts of Lyonesse and then open country.

Here he had to be more cautious. It was difficult stalking the spies with so much of the dusky road illuminated by warning lights. He wasn't suicidal enough to think of hiding in radiation pits. He hung back in an agony of indecision and was at last relieved to see them turn off the broken road and enter the old Baker farmhouse.

"Ah-ha!" said Addyer.

He sat down at the edge of the road on the remnants of a missile and asked himself: "Ah-ha what?" He could not answer, but he knew where to find the answer. He waited until dusk deepened to darkness and then slowly wormed his way forward toward the farmhouse.

It was while he was creeping between the deadly radiation glows and only occasionally butting his head against gravemarkers that he first became aware of two figures in the night. They were in the barnyard of the Baker place and were performing most peculiarly. One was tall and thin. A man. He stood stockstill, like a lighthouse. Upon occasion he took a slow, stately step with infinite caution and waved an arm in slow motion to the other figure. The second was also a man. He was stocky, and trotted jerkily back and forth.

As Addyer approached, he heard the tall man say: "Rooo booo fooo mooo hwaaa looo fooo."

Whereupon the trotter chattered: "Wd-nk-kd-ik-md-pd-ld-nk."

Then they both laughed; the tall man like a locomotive, the trotter like a chipmunk. They turned. The trotter rocketed into the house. The tall man drifted in. And that was amazingly that.

"Oh-ho," said Addyer.

At that moment a pair of hands seized him and lifted him from the ground. Addyer's heart constricted. He had time for one convulsive spasm before something vague was pressed against his face. As he lost consciousness his last idiotic thought was of telescopes.

Can you spare price of solitary coffee for no-loafing unfortunate, honorable sir? Charity will blessings.

When Addyer awoke he was lying on a couch in a small whitewashed room. A gray-haired gentlemen with heavy features was seated at a desk alongside the couch, busily ciphering on bits of paper. The desk was cluttered with what appeared to be intricate time-tables. There was a small radio perched on one side.

"L-Listen . . ." Addyer began faintly.

"Just a minute, Mr. Addyer," the gentleman said pleasantly. He fiddled with the radio. A glow germinated in the middle of the room over a circular copper plate and coalesced into a girl. She was extremely nude and extremely attractive. She scurried to the desk, patted the gentleman's head with the speed of a pneumatic hammer. She laughed and chattered: "Wd-nk-tk-ik-lt-nk."

The gray-haired man smiled and pointed to the door. "Go outside and walk it off," he said. She turned and streaked through the door.

"It has something to do with temporal rates," the gentleman said to Addyer. "I don't understand it. When they come forward they've got accumulated momentum." He began ciphering again. "Why in the world did you have to come snooping, Mr. Addyer?"

"You're spies," Addyer said. "She was talking Chinese."

"Hardly. I'd say it was French. Early French. Middle fifteenth century."

"Middle fifteenth century!" Addyer exclaimed.

"That's what I'd say. You begin to acquire an ear for those stepped-up tempos. Just a minute, please."

He switched the radio on again. Another glow appeared and solidified into a nude man. He was stout, hairy and lugubrious. With exasperating slowness he said: "Mooo fooo blooo wawww hawww pooo."

The gray-haired man pointed to the door. The stout man departed in slow motion.

"The way I see it," the gray-haired man continued conversationally, "when they come back they're swimming against the time current. That slows 'em down. When they come forward, they're swimming with the current. That speeds 'em up. Of course, in any case it doesn't last longer than a few minutes. It wears off."

"What?" Addyer said. "Time travel?"

"Yes. Of course."

"That thing . . ." Addyer pointed to the radio. "A time machine?"

"That's the idea. Roughly."

"But it's too small."

The gray-haired man laughed.

"What is this place anyway? What are you up to?"

"It's a funny thing," the gray-haired man said. "Everybody used to speculate about time-travel. How it would be used for exploration, archaeology, historical and social research and so on. Nobody ever guessed what the real use would be. . . . Therapy."

"Therapy? You mean medical therapy?"

"That's right. Psychological therapy for the misfits who won't respond to any other cure. We let them emigrate Escape. We've set up stations every quarter century. Stations like this."

"I don't understand."

"This is an immigration office."

"Oh my God!" Addyer shot up from the couch. "Then you're the answer to the population increase. Yes? That's how I happened to notice it. Mortality's up so high and birth's down so low these days that your time-addition becomes significant. Yes?"

"Yes, Mr. Addyer."

"Thousands of you coming here. From where?"

"From the future, of course. Time travel wasn't developed until C/H 127. That's . . . oh say, 2505 A.D. your chronology. We didn't set up our chain of stations until C/H 189."

"But those fast-moving ones. You said they came forward from the past."

"Oh yes, but they're all from the future originally. They just decided they went too far back."

"Too far?"

The gray-haired man nodded and reflected. "It's amusing, the mistakes people will make. They become unrealistic when they read history. Lose contact with facts. Chap I knew . . . wouldn't be satisfied with anything less than Elizabethan times. 'Shakespeare,' he said. 'Good Queen Bess. Spanish Armada. Drake and Hawkins and Raleigh. Most virile period in history. The Golden Age. That's for me, I couldn't talk sense into him, so we sent him back. Too bad."

"Well?" Addyer asked.

"Oh, he died in three weeks. Drank a glass of water. Typhoid."

"You didn't inoculate him? I mean, the army when it sends men overseas always—"

"Of course we did. Gave him all the immunization we could. But diseases evolve and change too. New strains develop. Old strains disappear. That's what causes pandemics. Evidently our shots wouldn't take against the Elizabethan typhoid. Excuse me . . ."

Again the glow appeared. Another nude man appeared, chattered briefly and then whipped through the door. He almost collided with the nude girl who poked her head in, smiled and called in a curious accent: "Ie vous prie de me pardonner. Quy estoit cette gentilhomme?"

"I was right," the gray-haired man said. "That's Medieval French. They haven't spoken like that since Rabelais." To the girl he said, "Middle English, please. The American dialect."

"Oh. I'm sorry, Mr. Jelling. I get so damned fouled up with my linguistics. Fouled? Is that right? Or do they say—"

"Hey!" Addyer cried in anguish.

"They say it, but only in private these years. Not before strangers."

"Oh yes. I remember. Who was that gentleman who just left?"

"Peters."

"From Athens?"

"That's right."

"Didn't like it, eh?"

"Not much. Seems the Peripatetics didn't have plumbing."

"Yes. You begin to hanker for a modern bathroom after a while. Where do I get some clothes . . . or don't they wear clothes this century?"

"No, that's a hundred years forward. Go see my wife. She's in the outfitting room in the barn. That's the big red building."

The tall lighthouse-man Addyer had first seen in the farmyard suddenly manifested himself behind the girl. He was now dressed and moving at normal speed. He stared at the girl; she stared at him. "Splem!" they both cried. They embraced and kissed shoulders.

"St'u my rock-ribbering rib-rockery to heart the hearts two," the man said.

"Heart's too, argal, too heart," the girl laughed.

"Eh? Then you st'u too."

They embraced again and left.

"What was that? Future talk?" Addyer asked. "Shorthand?"

"Shorthand?" Jelling exclaimed in a surprised tone. "Don't you know rhetoric when you hear it? That was thirtieth century rhetoric, man. We don't talk anything else up there. Prosthesis, Diastole, Epergesis, Metabasis, Hendiadys . . . And we're all born scanning."

"You don't have to sound so stuck-up," Addyer muttered enviously. "I could scan too if I tried."

"You'd find it damned inconvenient trying at your time of life."

"What difference would that make?"

"It would make a big difference," Jelling said, "because you'd find that living is the sum of conveniences. You might think plumbing is pretty unimportant compared to ancient Greek philosophers. Lots of people do. But the fact is, we already know the philosophy. After a while you get tired of seeing the great men and listening to them expound the material you already know. You begin to miss the conveniences and familiar patterns you used to take for granted."

"That," said Addyer, "is a superficial attitude."

"You think so? Try living in the past by candlelight,

without central heating, without refrigeration, canned
foods, elementary drugs. . . . Or, future-wise, try living
with Berganlicks, the Twenty-Two Commandments. Duo-
decimal calendars and currency, or try speaking in meter,
planning and scanning each sentence before you talk . . .
and damned for a contemptible illiterate if you forget
yourself and speak spontaneously in your own tongue."

"You're exaggerating," Addyer said. "I'll bet there are
times where I could be very happy. I've thought about it
for years, and I—"

"Tcha!" Jelling snorted. "The great illusion. Name
one."

"The American Revolution."

"Pfui! No sanitation. No medicine. Cholera in Philadelphia. Malaria in New York. No anesthesia. The death
penalty for hundreds of small crimes and petty infractions. None of the books and music you like best. None
of the jobs or professions for which you've been trained.
Try again."

"The Victorian Age."

"How are your teeth and eyes? In good shape? They'd
better be. We can't send your inlays and spectacles back
with you. How are your ethics? In bad shape? They'd better be or you'd starve in that cutthroat era. How do you
feel about class distinctions? They were pretty strong in
those days. What's your religion? You'd better not be a
Jew or Catholic or Quaker or Moravian or any minority.
What's your politics? If you're a reactionary today the
same opinions would make you a dangerous radical a
hundred years ago. I don't think you'd be happy."

"I'd be safe."

"Not unless you were rich; and we can't send money
back. Only the flesh. No, Addyer, the poor died at the
average age of forty in those days . . . worked out, worn
out. Only the privileged survived and you wouldn't be
one of the privileged."

"Not with my superior knowledge?"

Jelling nodded wearily. "I knew *that* would come up
sooner or later. What superior knowledge? Your hazy
recollection of science and invention? Don't be a damned
fool, Addyer. You enjoy your technology without the
faintest idea of how it works."

"It wouldn't have to be hazy recollection. I could
prepare."

"What, for instance?"

"Oh . . . say, the radio. I could make a fortune inventing the radio."

Jelling smiled. "You couldn't invent radio until you'd first invented the hundred allied technical discoveries that went into it. You'd have to create an entire new industrial world. You'd have to discover the vacuum rectifier and create an industry to manufacture it; the self-heterodyne circuit, the nonradiating neutrodyne receiver and so forth. You'd have to develop electric power production and transmission and alternating current. You'd have to—but why belabor the obvious? Could you invent internal combustion before the development of fuel oils?"

"My God!" Addyer groaned.

"And another thing," Jelling went on grimly. "I've been talking about technological tools, but language is a tool too; the tool of communication. Did you ever realize that all the studying you might do could never teach you how a language was really used centuries ago? Do you know how the Romans pronounced Latin? Do you know the Greek dialects? Could you learn to speak and think in Gaelic, seventeenth century Flemish, Old Low German? Never. You'd be a deaf-mute."

"I never thought about it that way," Addyer said slowly.

"Escapists never do. All they're looking for is a vague excuse to run away."

"What about books? I could memorize a great book and—"

"And what? Go back far enough into the past to anticipate the real author? You'd be anticipating the public too. A book doesn't become great until the public's ready to understand it. It doesn't become profitable until the public's ready to buy it."

"What about going forward into the future?" Addyer asked.

"I've already told you. It's the same problem only in reverse. Could a medieval man survive in the twentieth century? Could he stay alive in street traffic? Drive cars? Speak the language? Think in the language? Adapt to the tempo, ideas and coordinations you take for granted? Never. Could someone from the twenty-fifth century adapt to the thirtieth? Never."

"Well then," Addyer said angrily, "if the past and future are so uncomfortable, what are those people travelling around for?"

"They're not travelling," Jelling said. "They're running."

"From what?"

"Their own time."

"Why?"

"They don't like it."

"Why not?"

"Do you like yours? Does any neurotic?"

"Where are they going?"

"Any place but where they belong. They keep looking for the Golden Age. Tramps! Time-stiffs! Never satisfied. Always searching, shifting . . . bumming through the centuries. Pfui! Half the panhandlers you meet are probably time-bums stuck in the wrong century."

"And those people coming here . . . they think *this* is a Golden Age?"

"They do."

"They're crazy," Addyer protested. "Have they seen the ruins? The radiation? The war? The anxiety? The hysteria?"

"Sure. That's what appeals to them. Don't ask me why. Think of it this way: You like the American Colonial period, yes?"

"Among others."

"Well, if you told Mr. George Washington the reasons why you liked his time, you'd probably be naming everything he hated about it."

"But that's not a fair comparison. This is the worst age in all history."

Jelling waved his hand. "That's how it looks to you. Everybody says that in every generation; but take my word for it, no matter when you live and how you live, there's always somebody else somewhere else who thinks you live in the Golden Age."

"Well I'll be damned," Addyer said.

Jelling looked at him steadily for a long moment. "You will be," he said sorrowfully. "I've got bad news for you, Addyer. We can't let you remain. You'll talk and make trouble, and our secret's got to be kept. We'll have to send you out one-way."

"I can talk wherever I go."

"But nobody'll pay attention to you outside your own

time. You won't make sense. You'll be an eccentric . . .
a lunatic . . . a foreigner . . . safe."

"What if I come back?"

"You won't be able to get back without a visa, and
I'm not tattooing any visa on you. You won't be the first
we've had to transport, if that's any consolation to you.
There was a Jap, I remember—"

"Then you're going to send me somewhere in time?
Permanently?"

"That's right. I'm really very sorry."

"To the future or the past?"

"You can take your choice. Think it over while you're
getting undressed."

"You don't have to act so mournful," Addyer said. "It's
a great adventure. A high adventure. It's something I've
always dreamed."

"That's right. It's going to be wonderful."

"I could refuse," Addyer said nervously.

Jelling shook his head. "We'd only drug you and send
you anyway. It might as well be your choice."

"It's a choice I'm delighted to make."

"Sure. That's the spirit, Addyer."

"Everybody says I was born a hundred years too soon."

"Everybody generally says that . . . unless they say you
were born a hundred years too late."

"Some people say that too."

"Well, think it over. It's a permanent move. Which
would you prefer . . . the phonetic future or the poetic
past?"

Very slowly Addyer began to undress, as he undressed
each night when he began the prelude to his customary
fantasy. But now his dreams were faced with fulfillment
and the moment of decision terrified him. He was a little
blue and rather unsteady on his legs when he stepped
to the copper disc in the center of the floor. In answer to
Jelling's inquiry he muttered his choice. Then he turned
argent in the aura of an incandescent glow and disappeared from his time forever.

Where did he go? You know. I know. Addyer knows.
Addyer travelled to the land of Our pet fantasy. He
escaped into the refuge that is Our refuge, to the time
of Our dreams; and in practically no time at all he realized that he had in truth departed from the only time for
himself.

Through the vistas of the years every age but our own

seems glamorous and golden. We yearn for the yester-days and tomorrows, never realizing that we are faced with Hobson's Choice . . . that today, bitter or sweet, anxious or calm, is the only day for us. The dream of time is the traitor, and we are all accomplices to the betrayal of ourselves.

Can you spare price of one coffee, honorable sir? No, sir, I am not panhandling organism. I am starveling Japanese transient stranded in this so-miserable year. Honorable sir! I beg in tears for holy charity. Will you donate to this destitute person one ticket to township of Lyonesse? I want to beg on knees for visa. I want to go back to year 1945 again. I want to be in Hiroshima again. I want to go home.

✳

The Die-Hard

"IN THE OLD DAYS," THE OLD ONE SAID, "THERE WAS the United States and Russia and England and Russia and Spain and England and the United States. Countries. Sovereign States. Nations. Peoples of the world."

"Today there are peoples of the world, Old One."

"Who are you?" the Old One asked suddenly.

"I'm Tom."

"Tom?"

"No, Old One. Tom."

"I said Tom."

"You did not pronounce it properly, Old One. You spoke the name of another Tom."

"You are all Tom," the Old One said sullenly. "Everyone is Tom, Dick or Harry."

He sat, shaking in the sunshine, and hating the pleasant young man. They were on the broad veranda outside his hospital room. The street before them was packed with attractive men and women, all waiting expectantly. Somewhere in the white city there was a heavy cheering, a thrilling turmoil that slowly approached.

"Look at them." The Old One shook his cane at the street. "All Tom, and Dick and Harry. All Daisy, Anne and Mary."

"No, Old One," Tom smiled. "We use other names as well."

"I've had a hundred Toms sitting with me," the Old One snarled.

"We often use the same name, Old One, but we pronounce it differently. I'm not Tom or Tom or Tom. I'm Tom. Do you hear it?"

"What's that noise?" the Old One asked.

"It's the Galactic Envoy," Tom explained again. "The Envoy from Sirius, the star in Orion. He's touring the city. This is the first time a being from other worlds has ever visited the earth. There's great excitement."

"In the old days," the Old One said, "we had real envoys. Men from Paris and Rome and Berlin and London and Paris and— They came with pomp and circumstance. They made war. They made peace. Uniforms and guns and ceremonies. Brave times! Exciting times!"

"We have brave, exciting times today, Old One."

"You do not," the Old One snarled. He thumped his cane feebly. "There is no passion, no love, no fear, no death. There is no hot blood coursing through veins. You're all logic. All calm thought. All Tom, Dick and Harry."

"No, Old One. We love. We have passions. We fear many things. What you miss is the evil we have destroyed in ourselves."

"You have destroyed everything! You have destroyed man!" the Old One cried. He pointed a shaking finger at Tom. "You! How much blood have you in your veins?"

"None at all, Old One. I have Tamar's Solution in my veins. Blood cannot withstand radiation and I do my research in the Fission Piles."

"No blood," the Old One cackled. "And no bones either."

"Not all have been replaced, Old One."

"And no nerve tissue, heh?"

"Not all has been replaced, Old One."

"No blood, no bones, no guts, no heart. And no private parts. What do you do with a woman? How much of you is mechanical?"

"Not more than 60 per cent, Old One," Tom laughed. "I have children."

"And the other Toms and Dicks and Harrys?"

"Anywhere from 30 to 70 per cent, Old One. They have children, too. What the men of your time did to teeth, we do with all the body. There is no harm."

"You are not men! You're machines!" the Old One cried. "Robots! Monsters! You have destroyed man."

Tom smiled. "In truth, Old One, there is so much mingling of man in machine and machine in man that the distinction is hard to make. We no longer make it. We are content to live happily and work happily. We are adjusted."

"In the old days," the Old One said, "we all had real bodies. Blood and bones and nerves and guts. Like me. We worked and sweated and loved and fought and killed and lived. You do not live . . . you adjusted supermen . . . machine-men . . . half-bred bastards of acid and sperm. Nowhere have I seen a blow struck, a kiss taken, the clash of conflict, life. How I yearn to see real life again . . . not your machine imitation."

"That's the ancient sickness, Old One," Tom said seriously. "Why don't you let us reconstruct you and heal you? If you would let us replace your ductless glands, recondition your reflexes, and—"

"No! No! No!" the Old One cried in a high passion. "I will not become another Tom." He lurched up from his chair and beat at the pleasant young man with his cane. The blow broke the skin on the young man's face and was so unexpected that he cried out in astonishment. Another pleasant young man ran out on the veranda, seized the Old One and reseated him in his chair. Then he turned to Tom who was dabbing at the frosty liquid that oozed from the cut in his face.

"All right, Tom?"

"No great harm done." Tom looked at the Old One with awe. "Do you know, I believe he actually wanted to hurt me."

"Of course he did. This is your first time with him, isn't it? You ought to see him curse and carry on. What an old unreconstructed rebel he is. We're rather proud of the old boy. He's unique. A museum of pathology." The second young man sat down alongside the Old One. "I'll take him for a while. You go watch for the Envoy."

The Old One was shaking and weeping. "In the old days," he quavered, "there was courage and bravery and spirit and strength and red blood and courage and bravery and—"

"Now then, now then, Old One," his new companion interrupted briskly, "we have them too. When we reconstruct a man we don't take anything away from him but the rot in his mind and body."

"Who are you?" the Old One asked.

"I'm Tom."

"Tom?"

"No. Tom. Not Tom. Tom."

"You've changed."

"I'm not the same Tom that was here before."

"You're all Toms," the Old One cried piteously. "You're all the same God-forsaken Toms."

"No, Old One. We're all different. You just can't see it."

The turmoil and the cheering came closer. Out in the street before the hospital, the crowd began shouting in excited anticipation. A lane cleared. Far down the street there was a glitter of brass and the first pulse of the approaching music. Tom took the Old One under the arm and raised him from his chair.

"Come to the railing, Old One," he said excitedly. "Come and watch the Envoy. This is a great day for Mother Earth. We've made contact with the stars at last. It's a new era beginning."

"It's too late," the Old One muttered. "Too late."

"What do you mean, Old One?"

"We should have found them, not them us. We should have been first. In the old days we would have been first. In the old days there was courage and daring. We fought and endured. . . ."

"There he is," Tom shouted, pointing down the street. "He's stopped at the Institute . . . . Now he's coming out. . . . He's coming closer. . . . No. Wait! He's stopped again. . . . At the Center. What a magnificent gesture. This isn't just a token tour. He's inspecting everything."

"In the old days," the Old One mumbled, "we would have come with fire and storm. We would have marched down strange streets with weapons on our hips and defiance in our eyes. Or if they came first we would have met them with strength and defiance. But not you . . . machine half-breeds . . . laboratory supermen . . . adjusted . . . reconstructed . . . worthless. . . ."

"He's come out of the Center," Tom exclaimed. "He's coming closer. Look well, Old One. Never forget this moment. He—" Tom stopped and took a shuddering breath. "Old One," he said. "He's going to stop at the hospital!"

The gleaming car stopped before the hospital. The band marked time, still playing lustily, joyfully. The crowd roared. In the car the officials were smiling, pointing, explaining. The Galactic Envoy arose to his full, fantastic height, stepped out of the car and strode toward the steps leading up to the veranda. His escort followed.

"Here he comes!" Tom yelled, and began a confused roaring of his own.

Suddenly the Old One broke away from the railing. He shoved past Tom and all the other Tom, and Dick and Harrys and Daisy, Anne and Marys crowding the veranda. He beat his way through them with his feeble, wicked cane and came face to face with the Galactic Envoy at the head of the steps. He stared at the Praying Mantis face with horror and revulsion for one instant, then he cried: "I greet you. I alone can greet you."

He raised his cane and smote the face with all his strength.

"I'm the last man on earth," he cried.

✳

Of Time and Third Avenue

WHAT MACY HATED ABOUT THE MAN WAS THE FACT that he squeaked. Macy didn't know if it was the shoes, but he suspected the clothes. In the back room of his tavern, under the poster that asked: WHO FEARS MENTION THE BATTLE OF THE BOYNE? Macy inspected the stranger. He was tall, slender, and very dainty. Although he was young, he was almost bald. There was fuzz on top of his head and over his eyebrows. Then he reached into his jacket for a wallet, and Macy made up his mind. It was the clothes that squeaked.

"MQ, Mr. Macy," the stranger said in a staccato voice. "Very good. For rental of this backroom including exclusive utility for one chronos—"

"One whatos?" Macy asked nervously.

"Chronos. The incorrect word? Oh yes. Excuse me. One hour."

"You're a foreigner," Macy said. "What's your name? I bet it's Russian."

"No. Not foreign," the stranger answered. His frightening eyes whipped around the back room. "Identify me as Boyne."

"Boyne!" Macy echoed incredulously.

"MQ. Boyne." Mr. Boyne opened a wallet shaped like an accordion, ran his fingers through various colored papers and coins, then withdrew a hundred-dollar bill. He jabbed it at Macy and said: "Rental fee for one hour. As agreed. One hundred dollars. Take it and go."

Impelled by the thrust of Boyne's eyes, Macy took the bill and staggered out to the bar. Over his shoulder he quavered: "What'll you drink?"

"Drink? Alcohol? Pfui!" Boyne answered.

He turned and darted to the telephone booth, reached under the pay phone and located the lead-in wire. From a side pocket he withdrew a small glittering box and clipped it to the wire. He tucked it out of sight, then lifted the receiver.

"Coordinates West 73-58-15," he said rapidly, "North 40-45-20. Disband sigma. You're ghosting . . ." After a pause he continued: "Stet. Stet! Transmission clear. I want a fix on Knight. Oliver Wilson Knight. Probability to four significant figures. You have the coordinates. . . . 99.9807? MQ. Stand by. . . ."

Boyne poked his head out of the booth and peered toward the tavern door. He waited with steely concentration until a young man and a pretty girl entered. Then he ducked back to the phone. "Probability fulfilled. Oliver Wilson Knight in contact. MQ. Luck my Para." He hung up and was sitting under the poster as the couple wandered toward the back room.

The young man was about twenty-six, of medium height and inclined to be stocky. His suit was rumpled, his seal-brown hair was rumpled, and his friendly face was crinkled by good-natured creases. The girl had black hair, soft blue eyes, and a small private smile. They walked arm in arm and liked to collide gently when they thought no one was looking. At this moment they collided with Mr. Macy.

"I'm sorry, Mr. Knight," Macy said. "You and the young lady can't sit back there this afternoon. The premises have been rented."

Their faces fell. Boyne called: "Quite all right, Mr. Macy. All correct. Happy to entertain Mr. Knight and friend as guests."

Knight and the girl turned to Boyne uncertainly. Boyne smiled and patted the chair alongside him. "Sit down," he said. "Charmed, I assure you."

The girl said: "We hate to intrude, but this is the only place in town where you can get genuine Stone gingerbeer."

"Already aware of the fact, Miss Clinton." To Macy he said: "Bring gingerbeer and go. No other guests. These are all I'm expecting."

Knight and the girl stared at Boyne in astonishment as they sat down slowly. Knight placed a wrapped parcel of books on the table. The girl took a breath and said: "You know me . . . Mr. . . ?"

"Boyne. As in Boyne, Battle of. Yes, of course. You are Miss Jane Clinton. This is Mr. Oliver Wilson Knight. I rented premises particularly to meet you this afternoon."

"This supposed to be a gag?" Knight asked, a dull flush appearing on his cheeks.

"Gingerbeer," answered Boyne gallantly as Macy arrived, deposited bottles and glasses, and departed in haste.

"You couldn't know we were coming here," Jane said. "We didn't know ourselves . . . until a few minutes ago."

"Sorry to contradict, Miss Clinton," Boyne smiled. "The probability of your arrival at Longitude 73-58-15 Latitude 40-45-20 was 99.9807 per cent. No one can escape four significant figures."

"Listen," Knight began angrily, "if this is your idea of—"

"Kindly drink gingerbeer and listen to my idea, Mr. Knight." Boyne leaned across the table with galvanic intensity. "This hour has been arranged with difficulty and much cost. To whom? No matter. You have placed us in an extremely dangerous position. I have been sent to find a solution."

"Solution for what?" Knight asked.

Jane tried to rise. "I . . . I think we'd b-better be go—"

Boyne waved her back, and she sat down like a child. To Knight he said: "This noon you entered premises of J. D. Craig & Co., dealer in printed books. You purchased, through transfer of money, four books. Three do not matter, but the fourth . . ." He tapped the wrapped parcel emphatically. "That is the crux of this encounter."

"What the hell are you talking about?" Knight exclaimed.

"One bound volume consisting of collected facts and statistics."

"The Almanac?"

"The Almanac."

"What about it?"

"You intended to purchase a 1950 Almanac."

"I bought the '50 Almanac."

"You did not!" Boyne blazed. "You bought the Almanac for 1990."

"What?"

"The World Almanac for 1990," Boyne said clearly, "is in this package. Do not ask how. There was a carelessness that has already been disciplined. Now the error must be adjusted. That is why I am here. It is why this meeting was arranged. You cognate?"

Knight burst into laughter and reached for the parcel. Boyne leaned across the table and grasped his wrist. "You must not open it, Mr. Knight."

"All right." Knight leaned back in his chair. He grinned at Jane and sipped gingerbeer. "What's the payoff on the gag?"

"I must have the book, Mr. Knight. I would like to walk out of this tavern with the Almanac under my arm."

"You would, eh?"

"I would."

"The 1990 Almanac?"

"Yes."

"If," said Knight, "there was such a thing as a 1990 Almanac, and if it was in that package, wild horses couldn't get it away from me."

"Why, Mr. Knight?"

"Don't be an idiot. A look into the future? Stock market reports . . . Horse races . . . Politics. It'd be money from home. I'd be rich."

"Indeed yes." Boyne nodded sharply. "More than rich. Omnipotent. The small mind would use the Almanac from the future for small things only. Wagers on the outcome of games and elections. And so on. But the intellect of dimensions . . . *your* intellect . . . would not stop there."

"You tell me," Knight grinned.

"Deduction. Induction. Inference." Boyne ticked the points off on his fingers. "Each fact would tell you an entire history. Real estate investment, for example. What lands to buy and sell. Population shifts and census reports would tell you. Transportation. Lists of marine disasters and railroad wrecks would tell you whether rocket travel had replaced the train and ship."

"Has it?" Knight chuckled.

"Flight records would tell you which company's stock should be bought. Lists of postal receipts would indicate the cities of the future. The Nobel Prize winners would tell you which scientists and what new inventions to watch. Armament budgets would tell you what factories and industries to control. Cost-of-living reports would tell you how best to protect your wealth against inflation or deflation. Foreign exchange rates, stock exchange reports, bank suspensions and life insurance indexes would provide the clues to protect you against any and all disasters."

"That's the idea," Knight said. "That's for me."

"You really think so?"

"I know so. Money in my pocket. The world in my pocket."

"Excuse me," Boyne said keenly, "but you are only repeating the dreams of childhood. You want wealth. Yes. But only won through endeavor . . . your own endeavor. There is no joy in success as an unearned gift. There is nothing but guilt and unhappiness. You are aware of this already."

"I disagree," Knight said.

"Do you? Then why do you work? Why not steal? Rob? Burgle? Cheat others of their money to fill your own pockets?"

"But I—" Knight began, and then stopped.

"The point is well taken, eh?" Boyne waved his hand impatiently. "No, Mr. Knight. Seek a mature argument. You are too ambitious and healthy to wish to steal success."

"Then I'd just want to know if I would be successful."

"Ah? Stet. You wish to thumb through the pages looking for your name. You want reassurance. Why? Have you no confidence in yourself? You are a promising young attorney. Yes, I know that. It is part of my data. Has not Miss Clinton confidence in you?"

"Yes," Jane said in a loud voice. "He doesn't need reassurance from a book."

"What else, Mr. Knight?"

Knight hesitated, sobering in the face of Boyne's overwhelming intensity. Then he said: "Security."

"There is no such thing. Life is danger. You can only find security in death."

"You know what I mean," Knight muttered. "The knowledge that life is worth planning. There's the Atom Bomb."

Boyne nodded quickly. "True. It is a crisis. But then, I'm here. The world will continue. I am proof."

"If I believe you."

"And if you do not?" Boyne blazed. "You do not lack security. You lack courage." He nailed the couple with a contemptuous glare. "There is in this country a legend of pioneer forefathers from whom you are supposed to inherit courage in the face of odds. D. Boone, E. Allen, S. Houston, A. Lincoln, G. Washington and others. Fact?"

"I suppose so," Knight muttered. "That's what we keep telling ourselves."

"And where is the courage in you? Pfui! It is only talk. The unknown terrifies you. Danger does not inspire you to fight, as it did D. Crockett; it makes you whine and reach for the reassurance in this book. Fact?"

"But the Atom-Bomb . . ."

"It is a danger. Yes. One of many. What of that? Do you cheat at Solhand?"

"Solhand?"

"Your pardon." Boyne reconsidered, impatiently snapping his fingers at the interruption to the white heat of his argument. "It is a game played singly against chance relationships in an arrangement of cards. I forget your noun. . . ."

"Oh!" Jane's face brightened. "Solitaire."

"Quite right. Solitaire. Thank you, Miss Clinton." Boyne turned his frightening eyes on Knight. "Do you cheat at Solitaire?"

"Occasionally."

"Do you enjoy games won by cheating?"

"Not as a rule."

"They are thisney, yes? Boring. They are tiresome. Pointless. Null-Coordinated. You wish you had won honestly."

"I suppose so."

"And you will suppose so after you have looked at this bound book. Through all your pointless life you will wish you had played honestly the game of life. You will verdash that look. You will regret. You will totally recall the pronouncement of our great poet-philospher Trynbyll who summed it up in one lightning, skazon line. *'The Future is Tekon,'* said Trynbyll. Mr. Knight, do not cheat. Let me implore you to give me the Almanac."

"Why don't you take it away from me?"

"It must be a gift. We can rob you of nothing. We can give you nothing."

"That's a lie. You paid Macy to rent this backroom."

"Macy was paid, but I gave him nothing. He will think he was cheated, but you will see to it that he is not. All will be adjusted without dislocation."

"Wait a minute. . . ."

"It has all been carefully planned. I have gambled on you, Mr. Knight. I am depending on your good sense. Let me have the Almanac. I will disband . . . reorient . . . and you will never see me again. Vorloss verdash! It will be a bar adventure to narrate for friends. Give me the Almanac!"

"Hold the phone," Knight said. "This is a gag. Remember? I—"

"Is it?" Boyne interrupted. "Is it? Look at me."

For almost a minute the young couple stared at the bleached white face with its deadly eyes. The half-smile left Knight's lips, and Jane shuddered involuntarily. There was chill and dismay in the back room.

"My God!" Knight glanced helplessly at Jane. "This can't be happening. He's got me believing. You?"

Jane nodded jerkily.

"What should we do? If everything he says is true we can refuse and live happily ever after."

"No," Jane said in a choked voice. "There may be money and success in that book, but there's divorce and death too. Give him the Almanac."

"Take it," Knight said faintly.

Boyne rose instantly. He picked up the package and went into the phone booth. When he came out he had three books in one hand and a smaller parcel made up of the original wrapping in the other. He placed the books on the table and stood for a moment, holding the parcel and smiling down.

"My gratitude," he said. "You have eased a precarious situation. It is only fair you should receive something in return. We are forbidden to transfer anything that might divert existing phenomena streams, but at least I can give you one token of the future."

He backed away, bowed curiously, and said: "My service to you both." Then he turned and started out of the tavern.

"Hey!" Knight called. "The token?"

"Mr. Macy has it," Boyne answered and was gone.

The couple sat at the table for a few blank moments like sleepers slowly awakening. Then, as reality began to return, they stared at each other and burst into laughter.

"He really had me scared," Jane said.

"Talk about Third Avenue characters. What an act. What'd he get out of it?"

"Well . . . he got your Almanac."

"But it doesn't make sense." Knight began to laugh again. "All that business about paying Macy but not giving him anything. And I'm supposed to see that he isn't cheated. And the mystery token of the future . . ."

The tavern door burst open and Macy shot through the saloon into the back room. "Where is he?" Macy shouted. "Where's the thief? Boyne, he calls himself. More likely his name is Dillinger."

"Why, Mr. Macy!" Jane exclaimed. "What's the matter?"

"Where is he?" Macy pounded on the door of the Men's Room. "Come out, ye blaggard!"

"He's gone," Knight said. "He left just before you got back."

"And you, Mr. Knight!" Macy pointed a trembling finger at the young lawyer. "You, to be party to thievery and racketeers. Shame on you!"

"What's wrong?" Knight asked.

"He paid me one hundred dollars to rent this back room," Macy cried in anguish. "One hundred dollars. I took the bill over to Bernie the pawnbroker, being cautious-like, and he found out it's a forgery. It's a counterfeit."

"Oh no," Jane laughed. "That's too much. Counterfeit?"

"Look at this," Mr. Macy shouted, slamming the bill down on the table.

Knight inspected it closely. Suddenly he turned pale and the laughter drained out of his face. He reached into his inside pocket, withdrew a checkbook and began to write with trembling fingers.

"What on earth are you doing?" Jane asked.

"Making sure that Macy isn't cheated," Knight said.
"You'll get your hundred dollars, Mr. Macy."

"Oliver! Are you insane? Throwing away a hundred
dollars . . ."

"And I won't be losing anything either," Knight answered. "All will be adjusted without dislocation! They're
diabolical. Diabolical!"

"I don't understand."

"Look at the bill," Knight said in a shaky voice. "Look
closely."

It was beautifully engraved and genuine in appearance. Benjamin Franklin's benign features gazed up at
them mildly and authentically; but in the lower right-
hand corner was printed: Series 1980 D. And underneath that was signed: Oliver Wilson Knight, Secretary
of the Treasury.